# *Dinosaur Murder*

## By Patricia Bernard

Writers Exchange E-Publishing
http://www.writers-exchange.com

Dinosaur Murder
Copyright 2016, 2024, 2025 Patricia Bernard
Writers Exchange E-Publishing
PO Box 372
ATHERTON  QLD  4883

Cover Art by: Sandy Cummins

Published by Writers Exchange E-Publishing
http://www.writers-exchange.com

# Contents


| | |
|---|---|
| Chapter 1 | 1 |
| Chapter 2 | 11 |
| Chapter 3 | 24 |
| Chapter 4 | 46 |
| Chapter 5 | 57 |
| Chapter 6 | 72 |
| Chapter 7 | 86 |
| Chapter 8 | 100 |
| Chapter 9 | 114 |
| Chapter 10 | 130 |
| Chapter 11 | 144 |
| Chapter 12 | 154 |
| About the Author | 159 |
| Dinosaur Murder | 162 |
| Giant Stolen Cheesecake | 163 |
| Outcast Trilogy | 164 |
| The Mask | 166 |
| We Are Tam | 167 |

# *Chapter 1*

The floater, as Damien whisperingly called it, drifted closer. Two more rippling waves and it would bump into Abba. She edged away, the pool was small and there was no more room on their submerged ledge.

"Can you see it?" shouted a voice.

"No," yelled the man who was standing immediately above them on the overhanging rock.

Abba wondered if he was the man they'd seen hit the floater with a hammer and continue hitting him as he stumbled across the rocks and into the sea.

She held her breath as the floater's pudgy hand bobbed closer to her bare arm. It was the same colour as her T-shirt, a washed-out yellow. Suntan, her mind automatically registered. He's a local.

Then, as the floater swivelled round in the current and bobbed straight towards her, she stepped off the ledge and trod water so that its longish hair wouldn't streak across her face.

A wave splashed over her, filling her mouth with salty water, and for the hundredth time she asked herself why she had been so stupid as to offer to show her biggest secret to Jimmy Chadwick - someone she'd met on the Internet, and who she had only met in the flesh two days ago. And why, oh why, hadn't she backed out when he'd brought along snobby Damian.

But she knew why and neither reason was one to be proud of. She had wanted to show off to Jimmy because he knew so much about Dinosaurs, her most favourite subject on earth: and because he'd offered to send her copies of his pterosaur fossil photographs once he returned to Sydney. Pterosaurs, with their hairy reptile bodies and bat-like wings, were her favourite dinos. So how could she not try to impress Jimmy? He was so cute with his earnest grey eyes and sticking-up blonde hair.

As for Damian, with his floppy hair, labelled jeans, ironed Mambo T-shirt and snobby way of saying 'It's Damian with one M, not two', the only reason she'd agreed to let him come was because she'd suddenly had the idea that by being nice to him, his father might help her mother get a better job. She wasn't sure how, but the enormous mining company that the all-powerful Padres East worked for also owned the string of hotels, which included the Broome Summon Hotel where her mother worked as night receptionist, so it was worth a try.

Of course, everything had gone wrong. Just as her grandfather would have predicted if he had known what she was up to. She could hear his voice in her ear as another froth-filled wave splashed over her. "Abba. Abba. Abba, you do something for the wrong reasons and the wrong reason will punch you in the face."

Which, she thought as a third wave slapped her in the face, was exactly what had happened from the moment they'd taken the hotel's bicycles in the middle of the night without telling anyone. First Damien had buckled his bike's wheel, then they'd seen a murder, and now they were neck deep in water with a very good chance of the man with the torch seeing them. A torch beam pierced the darkness, barely missing the floater and Abba's dark curly hair.

Jimmy grabbed her T-shirt and heaved her back onto the ledge just as the incoming tide pushed the floater up against them. Damian pushed it away, but it persistently returned, nudging them in a friendly way as if it too wanted to remain hidden in the deep shadow of the rocks, away from the brutal men above.

Jimmy gagged noisily as the body's gym shoe hooked around his neck. Abba stared at him, as if the very size of her shocked black eyes would stop him making a noise. It did.

After a few seconds, which felt like hours for the submerged teenagers, the man with the torch moved away and Damian pushed the body out to sea again.

The rock pool was filling fast. Soon their mouths would be covered and they would have to swim for it. Swimming was not Jimmy's best sport; in fact no sport was; but swimming in the open sea was his worst.

"Are you sure there are no saltwater crocs this far south?" he whispered.

"Not normally," Abba whispered back. "They hang out around the earl farms further north."

"Which is about fifteen kilometres away," added Damien. "A mere skip and a jump for the average four metre estuarine croc--who has been known to swim hundreds of kilometres."

Jimmy stared at Damien. It was the first time he had heard him say anything the slightest bit knowledgeable.

"Shut up Damien, you're frightening him," Abba hissed.

"I'm not fir..."

"Have you found him?" shouted a voice so close that it shocked the teenagers into silence.

"No. He's probably halfway to India," answered a second voice, from just above their heads.

"And good riddance, the thieving turd," answered the first.

"Zen let us get to work," yelled a third voice from further away. "Ze tide is coming in."

"What if he isn't dead?" shouted the closest man.

"Then he soon will be. Now hurry up."

The teenagers listened to the two men's footsteps as they scrambled back over the gravel and rocks. A few minutes later the hammering and sawing started. Abba counted twenty muted thumps before whispering. "I think we can get out of here now."

Jimmy held his camera under her nose. "I can't swim and keep my camera dry at the same time. It's not an underwater camera."

"Give it to me, I can."

Abba waited until a wave was coming in then she launched herself into the frothy black water, breast-stroking with one arm, while holding the camera above her head with the other. Four strokes and she'd reached a flat, accessible rock. Jimmy came next, splashing too loudly, she thought, as she hauled him up beside her.

Next came Damian, gliding through the water like a fish. But of course, she thought resentfully, that is exactly how Damien East would swim. His posh private school probably had individual swimming instructors. Pity they didn't give him bike-riding lessons. Her mother was going to be furious about the hotel bike's buckled wheel.

Damien hoisted himself up beside Jimmy. Behind them the body rocked like a piece of driftwood, its arms outstretched and its bruised face facing the sea-urchin-strewn sea floor. He pushed back his longish hair so it hooked behind his ears and whispered. "So what do you think will happen to him...it?"

Abba shrugged slightly. "It'll be sucked out into the ocean and most likely never be seen again."

"But that's not right. He's been murdered. Someone has to catch the murderer," said Jimmy forgetting to keep his voice low.

"Did you hear that?" demanded a voice, not as far away as Abba had thought it should be. "There is someone here."

The three held their breath.

"You're imagining things," came a curt answer.

Then the hammering began again.

Abba stretched up so she could see where the men were. They were close to where she had pulled away the seaweed and removed the rocks that she used to hide the four stegosaurus' fossilised footprints.

Jimmy had taken at least thirty photographs of the footprints before the tide began washing the seaweed back over them. Then they'd heard the men coming across the rocks. As they were in a National Park, and no one was supposed to be there at night --including themselves--they hid amongst the rocks, hoping the men were fishermen and that they would move on. They hadn't. Instead, they'd argued over money. One was demanding a larger share and threatening to tell someone if he didn't get it, when the taller one--the one with the white hair--bashed him with a hammer.

Now they were hammering and chiselling at the rock. But why? To secure the rope of a lobster pot or fish trap perhaps. But this wasn't the right place to lower a trap or pot, and the men weren't dressed like fishermen. Two were wearing long trousers and long-sleeved shirts. The only time Broome men dressed like that was when they were getting married or going to a funeral.

Abba bobbed down again. "Do we drag the floater up onto the rocks so that the sharks and fish can't mangle it before we escape and ring the police? Or do we get out of here fast, then ring the police and let them find it in the water, if they can?"

Damien couldn't believe his ears. *Why was this stupid girl wanting to get them involved in this mess? Couldn't she see they were already neck deep in sh... Trouble? How was he going to explain the buckled bicycle wheel? The stolen buckled bicycle wheel to be exact. How was he going to explain having left the Sunmoon Hotel when his father had thought he was watching a re-re-run of Star Wars in Jimmy's room? What lies was he going to have to invent to get himself out of this mess? Ringing the police was out of the question.*

"Or we don't ring the police," he hissed. "We aren't supposed to be here. Remember?"

Abba ignored him and raised her fine dark eyebrows questioningly at Jimmy.

Jimmy wasn't sure what she was asking. Was it: do we phone the police? Or was it why did you bring this whingeing woos along?

He'd already told her why when they'd bicycled ahead of Damien. His father had said that Damien's father had asked him if Damien could hang out with Jimmy while they were attending the same conference. Jimmy's father had said it would be a kind thing to do and that he would feel more comfortable about Jimmy going out so late with Abba if another boy was going along. As if going bike-riding with a girl was a date or something. Or even a girlfriend-boyfriend thing.

Jimmy knew that his father felt about the girlfriend-boyfriend thing, because two years ago on his fifteenth birthday he'd been given the divided-brain lecture. Which began with, "If a boy is thinking about girls all the time, he can't study," And ended with, "A divided brain cannot study successfully enough to pass exams, so your mother and I would prefer it you gave girls a miss until you finish high school matriculated and are enrolled in uni."

FINISH HIGH SCHOOL! THAT WAS TWO YEARS AWAY! He'd be ancient by then.

"So, if Damien East, goes can I go?" he'd asked again.

His father stopped revising his speech on why the proposed gas mining of the Murray-Darling Basin could destroy the local flora and fauna and focused his attention on Jimmy.

"Why do you have to start off so late?"

"Because that is the only time the tide is far enough out for the footprints to be seen. And even then, it is only a few times a year. We're lucky to be here now."

"How long will you be?"

"If we leave by eleven, we will be back by one."

"And this girl. How old is she? And how did you meet her?"

"She's seventeen and she's a fossil freak like me. In fact, she is the only one who knows where the footprints are. She discovered them while snorkelling for beche-de-mer. You know, those big sea worms that look like cucumbers? Her grandfather sells them to the Chinese."

"I know what a beche-de-mer looks like, Jimmy. I helped save them from over-harvesting. I thought only Aborigines were allowed to fish for them around here."

Jimmy spoke up quickly, worried that he'd gotten Abba into trouble. "Abba's grandmother was Aboriginal, which makes Abba one-quarter Aboriginal. Dad, honestly! Four matching stegosaurus footprints! It would be the best photograph ever!"

"You promise it isn't dangerous."

"It's as dangerous as going to the cinema."

"All right! But only if you take Damien along. And only if you are back by one."

So, although he didn't like Damien East much, Jimmy had asked him to come along; and Damien, who'd said he'd have to say he was watching videos in Jimmy's room, had agreed, but only because he was bored witless with the hotel.

When the boys met at 11'clock, Abba was not pleased to see Damien, mainly because within minutes it was clear he wasn't a good bike rider, and she showed it by her huffy silence. Then after he introduced himself as "Damien with one M, not two", and Abba said that her name was Abigail, but she preferred Abba because she was an ABBA music fan, at which he'd sneered, "How retro!" she decided that Damien with one M not two, was not on her best friend list and that she would ignore him.

Which she'd done successfully until they were riding towards Gantheaume Point and Damien rode into a huge rock and bucked his bike's front wheel. After that they'd wheeled the bikes along the sand-covered track towards Reddell Beach with Jimmy and Abba talking about dinosaurs and Damien following behind sighing loudly to show he was bored.

"He's a sulk," breathed Abba. "I wish you hadn't brought him."

Jimmy nodded. Staring down at the bobbing body, he wished that not only had he not brought Damien, but that he hadn't brought himself either.

"So," said Abba, taking their silence as agreeing with her idea of what they should do, "We'll drag the floater up onto the rocks and leave it under that ledge for the police to find. Only quietly, because sound travels."

"Which is a good reason for forgetting it and getting out of here," hissed Damien.

Abba frowned hard at him. "We will, once we have secured it."

"And once I have taken a photograph as proof," added Jimmy focussing his camera.

Damien's blue eyes looked almost silver in the moonlight as he grabbed Jimmy's arm. "Are you insane? They'll see the flash."

*He's scared. The posh Damien in his labelled clothes is scared stiff,* thought Abba as she put her hand on Damien's arm so he'd release Jimmy. Then she whispered in his ear. "Jimmy is right. We need proof. He can aim the camera out to sea that way the flash won't be seen."

Jimmy took the photograph. The flash sparkled and glimmered for a second over the oncoming waves as it joined the silver staircase of the moon's reflection and disappeared. Jimmy hung his camera around his neck and stretched his hand towards the body.

"Damien, take his feet."

"No way! Look, I only have to do one more thing wrong and my father's going to ship me off to London to live with my mum faster than I can blink."

Abba grabbed hold of the body's Hawaiian-print shirt, careful not to touch any skin, "My mum isn't going to be pleased to hear about me being here either, but he was a human being, and we can't leave him for the fish or crocs."

"That's fine for you to say. You aren't in danger of being sent to a stepfather who hates your guts and a mother who doesn't remember you are on the planet," muttered Damien grabbing hold of a soggy tennis shoe.

Abba barely heard his whingeing. She was thinking about how she did not want the body to roll over and stare at her with its glassy water-filled eyes. How, if its clammy cold skin touched hers, she'd faint. And how she wished she had never offered to show Jimmy Chadwick her secret.

"All together, pull," she urged softly.

Slowly, quietly, they dragged the body onto the rocks trying to avoid touching any fleshy parts. It wasn't easy. The gym shoe came off in Damien's hand. The sucking noise of the sea trying to pull the body back made them all shiver. And the dark slick of blood from the head wounds as they dragged it under an overhanging ledge made Jimmy gag again.

"If you chuck up, they'll hear you," warned Abba.

Jimmy swallowed great gups of air and didn't chuck up.

They were crawling across the rocks and Abba was about to suggest how they could get to the bikes without being seen when a torch beam lit up her face and a voice yelled. "There's someone here."

"Quick!!" screamed Abba as she scrambled over the rocks like a crab. "Get out of here."

Damien leapt after her, but Jimmy turned and photographed the running man climbing the rocks after them. The flash blinded him, so Jimmy took three more photographs. Then while the man stopped to blink and rub his eyes, Jimmy scrambled after Abba and Damien.

# *Chapter 2*

Abba and Damien slid and slithered over the wet and slippery tide-line rocks bashing their knees and elbows in their effort to escape.

Higher up the hill the volcanic stone became pitted and sharp, and the spiky moon grass that grew amongst the rocks stabbed Abba's bare legs and feet and hooked into Damien's tennis socks. Abba turned to see how close the torch-waving man was and realised that Jimmy wasn't behind them.

Abba pulled Damien down into a clump of saltbush as the torch beam flashed over their heads. "Jimmy must have run in another direction. Now slither like snakes."

She slid sideways down the hill, away from the torchlight and Damien realised, with a sinking feeling, that they were moving away from the bikes and the track back to town.

Damien slithered as best he could while trying to protect his new jeans and T-shirt, but it was useless. He snagged his T-shirt twice and he was sure he'd torn the knee out of his jeans. His father would be livid. Keeping one's clothes looking new and pristine-neat was one of Padric East's main obsessions. "Otherwise," he would say, while checking to see that his own suit was creaseless, "why buy new and expensive clothing? Why bother to put identity labels on them so they don't get lost at school or camp? Why not wear a hessian bag?"

Damien glanced ahead at Abba's faded flower print board shorts. They weren't exactly a hessian bag, but as far as his father was concerned, they might as well be. As for putting identity labels on them, that was a joke. Abba's public school probably didn't even have a uniform, whereas labels were compulsory on everything, even casual clothes, at his private school.

Abba slipped between two rocks and Damien was about to follow when something dry and scaly slid over his fingers. He snatched his hand back.

"Does Broome have carpet pythons like Darwin?" he hissed.

Abba didn't answer.

Damien comforted himself with the thought that pythons couldn't be half as dangerous as the man with the torch.

They were lying face down amongst the bushes so the torchlight couldn't pick up their eyes when they heard one of the men down by the shore shout, "Leave it. We'll get them later. They can't get far."

The man with the torch, who was so close they could hear his heavy breathing, turned back, and Abba and Damien wriggled uphill again.

"What about Jimmy?" grunted Damien.

Not that he cared a hoot about stupid Jimmy, whom he'd only talked to because his father had forced him to. "You're here for another three days, Damien, so learn to network. Networking is the basis of money making. Networking with people you don't like is a businessman's best tool. If you networked more at school, you'd be in a lot less trouble. And I did warn you before you came that I couldn't entertain you."

*As if,* thought Damien. *And as if I asked you to.*

So, Damien East had been introduced to dorky Jimmy Chadwick in his daggy shorts and out-of-date pink T-Shirt, and dorky Jimmy Chadwick had invited him to go on an eleven-o'clock bike ride. Now they were up to their necks in it, and if Jimmy got caught by the murderer, nothing Damien said--lies or truth--would save him from his father's threat to send him to London.

Abba tapped him on the shoulder. "Come on. Jimmy will know we are heading for the bikes."

Five minutes later they reached the track that ran along the cliffs of Reddell Beach. Abba poked her head above the bushes to see if it was safe to break cover. With a hiss of warning, she dropped to the ground gluing herself to the earth. Damien did the same as two men staggered up the hill carrying a heavy load in a blanket slug between them.

The men, panting and swearing at the weight of the blanket, passed so close that one glance to the left and Abba's pale T-shirt and shorts would have been seen amongst the silver saltbush: one step to the right and they would have walked on Damien's leg. Two minutes later the men reached the track, turned left and were out of sight and Abba and Damien could breathe again.

Abba waited for Damien to crawl up beside her, then she put her lips close to his ear. "It looked like a second body. What do you think?"

Damien shrugged. In his mind there was no doubt about it.

"Maybe the third man got cold feet about the floater, and they knocked him into the sea as well," she continued. "Their trousers were wet."

Damien didn't care how wet the men were. All he could think of was that they'd killed once so they wouldn't think twice about knocking two-stickybeak teenagers on the head.

"Let's get out of here."

He stood up, climbed onto the track, and raced away in the opposite direction to the men.

"It works for me," panted Abba, running after him.

They were jogging along the track when they heard an engine start up and a car driving off towards the lighthouse.

Damien stopped to listen, "They're taking the body somewhere else."

Abba, who was searching for where they left the bicycles, nodded back to him.

"I'm sure they were around here somewhere," she added.

"They were," said a voice they both knew as Jimmy pushed aside the bushes he'd been hiding behind. "But they were in full view, so I moved them. Then I hid because I thought you were the men."

With a cry of relief Abba flung her arms around the stocky blond boy and hugged him hard. "I was so worried about you. How did you get here so fast?"

"I blinded the man with my flash. Then, while he was stumbling in your direction, I doubled back and shot up the hill," He explained quickly, while wondering if he was supposed to hug her back. He hoped not. Hugging was something his sisters did all the time and something he avoided all the time.

Abba let go of him and began heaving her bike out of the scrub. "That was smart. I wouldn't have thought of that."

"How did you get past the other men?" asked Damien.

"They were busy cutting and digging into the rock."

Damien helped drag the other two bikes out of the bushes before he asked. "Did it look like they were digging up a body?"

"Out of the rock! No. Why?"

"We saw two of the men carrying something heavy wrapped in a blanket and the man with the torch was nowhere around," explained Abba.

"Wow!" breathed Jimmy. "This is one awesome night." Then he shook his head. "Only it couldn't have been the man with the torch. He came up to the road earlier and headed for their car."

"What sort of a car?" asked Damien, pushing his reluctant bike harder to keep up with the other two.

"An old Toyota utility without a number plate, but I couldn't take a photo because the torch man was in it, and he would have seen the flash."

"So, who was in the blanket?" demanded Abba.

"The floater! So now we don't have to ring the police, 'cause it's not there anymore," cried Damien triumphantly.

"A body is a body," said Jimmy, "I have a photograph to prove it and a photograph of one of the murderers."

"And they know it," Damien reminded him. "So, has it occurred to you that their ute might not have gone very far? Remember that voice shouting out that they'd get us later. What if they're parked somewhere waiting for us? Or the ute driving away was a red herring and they are doubling back right this minute?"

"That's why we are going in the opposite direction," said Abba.

"Wouldn't they expect us to go in the opposite direction? Couldn't that be a red herring too?"

Abba stopped pushing her bike. "Damien is right. We'll leave the busted bike hidden here and take the short cut that runs behind the racecourse. Once we're on the main road one of you can dink me. It's the long way but it's safer."

It took them an hour to push the bikes along the sandy track and to take turns dinking Abba along Kavite Road to Port Drive. They were congratulating themselves on having escaped when they heard the sound of a vehicle coming along the deserted road. As no vehicles had passed them so far, they stopped riding to listen.

"It's the Toyota ute," yelled Jimmy, bouncing down into the ditch and sending Abba and himself flying off the bike.

"Ouch! That hurt!" moaned Abba, crawling out of a clump of prickles.

"Ouch!" cried Jimmy crawling after her.

"Watch out!" warned Damien, as he bounced down behind them, just managing to keep his balance.

The ute drove slowly past their hiding place.

"How did you know it was the Toyota ute?" whispered Damien.

"All utes have a different sound," said Jimmy confidently. "Plus, that ute has a bald tyre on the back left side, and if you listen you can hear the uneven tread as the wheel goes around."

Damien stared hard at Jimmy. He could barely see him in the shadow of the ditch, "That's impossible."

"The bald tyre or hearing the bald tyre?" asked Abba.

"It's coming back," warned Jimmy.

The ute passed them again. They waited until they couldn't hear it anymore, then they pushed the bikes out of the ditch and pedalled on. This time Abba sat behind Damien as he pedalled her bike.

The ute returned twice, cruising by with its headlights off. The first time they hid behind someone's bougainvillea hedge. The second time they hid amongst the long grass by the side of the road. After that they turned off Port Drive and kept to the side streets until they reached Frederic Street.

"Stop! There's a public phone box. We have to ring the police," cried Abba.

"Who exactly is the *we* that you are talking about?" demanded Damien, as he braked, and she slipped off the back of the bike.

"Well, it can't be me," she told him. "The constable knows me and will recognise my voice. So, it will have to be one of you. You sound the oldest, Damien."

"No way!" he snapped. "I'm not supposed to be here. In fact. I'm invisible."

"I'll do it," said Jimmy, popping his bike beside the phone box. "But first, I'll have to disguise my voice."

Damien and Abba watched as he took off his T-shirt and stuffed a sleeve into each side of his mouth. "How do I sound," he asked.

Abba giggled. "Weird. Like a Christmas chipmunk."

"But no-one will recognise you," added Damien, who was feeling guilty about refusing to call the police so was being intentionally nice to Jimmy.

Abba dialled the number and handed the phone to Jimmy who was adjusting his T-shirt so he wouldn't choke. When the police answered he shouted into the phone. "There was a murder tonight, south of the lighthouse, on the rocks before Lurujarri Walk. Three men attacked a fourth man with a hammer. The body was hidden under a ledge. There is a slick of blood to prove it. Then the body was carried away in a blanket and put into a white Toyota utility with no numberplate."

"Who is this? State your name. Is this a practical joke? State your name please."

"Hang up," mouthed Abba.

They were cycling along Frederick Street when they saw the ute again. It was parked halfway across the road at the Cable Beach Road Junction. No-one could pass it without being seen. The bike riders pulled into the shadow of a tall palm.

"Do you think they saw us?" demanded Jimmy.

Abba peered at the distant ute. "Don't know, but they must know we're from one of the Cable Beach hotels otherwise, why park there?"

Damien voice rose in panic. "How would they know that?"

"Keep your voice down," warned Abba. "Sound carries at night."

"I am keeping it down," Damien hissed angrily.

"No, you're not," whispered Jimmy. "You're practically yelling."

Damien clenched his teeth and rounded on the blond boy. "Who do you think you are telling me what to do? You're just the son of an office worker. My dad could buy and sell you and your father."

"Oh, would that be the dad whose company wrecks farms and waterways for money and whose company wrecks beaches to mine sand?" retorted Jimmy just as angrily.

"Enough!" hissed Abba, "Both your fathers could buy and sell my father, and do I care? No! So, stop bickering like kindergarten kids and let me think."

Both boys fell silent, but continued to glare at each other, while Abba stared hard at the ute. Then she nodded. "Got it. I know a short cut that will bring us around to the other side of the Junction."

"What about them knowing we are at one of the Cable Beach hotels?" asked Jimmy.

"There are lots of hotels, and by tomorrow Broome will be crawling with police and they will have to stop looking for us."

"If the police didn't think Jimmy's funny voice phone call was a hoax," muttered Damien.

Jimmy glared at him, "If they do. I can always post them the photographs of the body and the torch man."

"No, you can't," argued Damien. "Any photographs printed out of a computer can be traced. The police would know within minutes who took them, and then my dad would find out about me lying about where I was tonight."

"Oh really! Would that be the dad who can buy and sell...?"

"Shut up! Jimmy!" ordered Abba. "Keep to the shadows and turn left at the first street."

"You mean walk closer to the ute?" demanded Damien.

"There are no streetlights, so as long as we make no noise, we should be safe."

With his eyes on the ute, Damien reluctantly followed the other two through the shadows to the side street. The ute didn't move. A block down the side street Abba turned onto a track that led behind a house. The noise of the bikes going through the long grass started a dog barking. A few minutes later Abba stopped at a wire fence.

"The posts don't meet at the end. Push the bikes through," she whispered as the dog barked louder and closer.

*Easier said than done*, thought Jimmy as he wrangled his bike through the small gap. Damien came behind him, scraping the hotel bike's paintwork on the wire.

Ahead of them stretched an acre of tall thin gravestones set out in long neat rows. The white and gold Japanese writing painted on the dark granite shone eerily in the moonlight, and there was a strange, sweet smell.

Jimmy made a face at the smell. "What is this place?"

"It's where the Japanese pearl divers were buried after they got the bends from being down so deep and they died coming up," answered Abba.

"And the smell?"

"The Japanese have a Matsuri Festival every year to commemorate the dead. What you can smell are the flowers and incense candles they left here six days ago."

"How many graves are there?"

"About a hundred."

"Sssshhh," warned Damien. "Someone's coming."

They stopped and listened. There was movement from two different directions. Abba gestured for the boys to pick up the bikes to minimise the noise, then to creep to the left. Damien heaved his bike onto his shoulder, while Jimmy and Abba lifted up the other. Then they crept through the lines of graves to the side fence.

"We should be able to slide under here," she whispered.

Behind them a torch beam flicked on and off as a stooped figure crept stealthily between the graves.

"He saw us on the road," breathed Damien, as Abba lifted the wire fencing for him to wriggle under, pulling the bike with him.

Jimmy went next, then Abba. She was halfway through when a huge black dog bounded out at her from behind a grave. Pouncing on her legs, it began to lick them.

"Get away," she hissed.

But the dog squeezed under the fence with her trying to lick her face.

She scrambled up, grabbed the bike from Jimmy and began pushing it as fast as she could towards some crooked tombstones. The dog loped along beside her, wagging its tail.

Jimmy avoided a fallen tombstone. "What's this place, Abba?"

"The Chinese Cemetery. It isn't as looked after as the Japanese one and doesn't have a fence, so it's easier to get out of."

As they rode away from the Chinese and Japanese Cemeteries with the friendly dog tagging along, they saw the torchlight swing round and begin coming back through the Japanese gravestones. "Pedal as fast as you can," urged Abba from the back of Jimmy's bike. "Before he realises we have got away.

Within minutes they'd turned into the street that joined up with Cable Beach Road East. Here they slowed down to catch their breath.

"He's a local," said Abba. "Otherwise, he wouldn't have known about the track through the Japanese Cemetery."

"What about the others?" asked Jimmy.

"The floater had a tan and a Hawaiian-print shirt so he could be local too. The others looked like city men."

"Which city?" asked Damien. "One of them had a foreign accent."

"Darwin, Perth, Sydney, Melbourne, Adelaide," recited Abba. "Take your pick. They all fly foreign tourists up here."

They were still discussing the ute, its driver, and the two city men as they cycled up the driveway of the Sunmoon Hotel.

Outside the bicycle shed Abba glanced at her watch and pulled a wry face. "We're an hour and a half late. Too late for me to go home so I'm going to collapse on the sofa in the staff lounge. What are you two going to do?"

"I'm going to creep into our room," said Jimmy. "If my dad wakes up I'm going to say that on the way back from seeing the stegosaurus footprints Damien crashed his bike so we had to walk home slowly because he was in pain. What about you Damien?"

"My dad will freak if he thinks I left the hotel, so I'm going to say I fell asleep in your room after we watched the videos. With a bit of luck our fathers are going to be so busy arguing about sand and gas mining versus flora and fauna that they won't check up on our different stories."

"Oh!" Abba smiled sweetly, "Would that be the argument you two have already had?"

Both boys looked sheepishly at each other, then they grinned.

"So, what do you reckon?" said Abba. "Will we meet here tomorrow at one o'clock? By then the police might have found the body and we'll be off the hook."

*Fat chance*, thought Damien, as he slowly twisted the key and softly pushed open the door to his father's hotel suite.

"No point in creeping in," said his father from his bedroom. "I'm wide awake and I know the time. Where have you been till this hour?"

The rehearsed lie of falling asleep in Jimmy's room was on the tip of Damien's tongue, when he remembered his father only asked direct questions when he already knew the answers, then he'd wait for Damien to lie so he could catch him out.

"We didn't watch videos," he said, stopping at the open bedroom door with his fingers crossed behind his back. "We went for a bike ride."

Across the room his father looked up from the laptop balanced on his knees. Then he rested back on a pile of pillows and took off his glasses.

"Go on."

"My bike, I mean the hotel's bike, hit a rock and buckled the front wheel so we had to walk home. It took ages."

Padric East made a pursed chewing movement with his lips, then he turned back to his computer. "Well at least you didn't lie about it. Although I bet Jimmy Chadwick's father a beer that you would."

Damien's heart leapt into his mouth. "I thought you didn't like Mr Chadwick? I thought he was the enemy."

His father didn't look up. "He is, Damien. But he's also a good debater, and I believe in networking, remember? He said that you two were off looking at dinosaur footprints. I said I was pretty sure he was mistaken. Dinosaur footprints not figuring high on your agenda. That pretty much nothing of educational value did. I'm glad to see I misjudged you."

Damien waited for an apology from his father about him being wrong, but none was forthcoming. *Don't expect it*, he thought.

His father turned off his computer and beckoned to him. "So how badly are you hurt? Let me see."

Damien sidled into the bedroom hoping that the bedside lamp wouldn't show up his torn jeans and T-shirt, but his father snapped on the overhead light.

"Good God! Your clothes are a mess!"

Damien decided not to mention how much his elbows and knees hurt.

# *Chapter 3*

Jimmy was the first to arrive at the bicycle shed. Then Abba. She was wearing another sun-bleached T-shirt and a brightly coloured fringed mini-sarong that showed off her long brown legs. Jimmy tried not to look at them.

Flicking back a mop of curls from her forehead she grinned at him. "Wasn't last night awesomely awful? I kept thinking about it all day. "

Jimmy grinned back. "Totally. I still can't believe it happened."

"There was nothing on the radio or TV this morning. Have you seen Damien?"

"No. I was sort of grounded with homework for coming in so late. I bet he was as well."

Abba wrinkled up her nose at the idea. "He seems pretty scared of his father. What's he like?"

Jimmy ran his fingers through his blond hair; spiked especially to impress Abba. "My dad says Mr. East is a killer businessman and that the World Wildlife Fund, who my dad works for, can't win against him. The best they can do is halt some of the damage. But that's only because Dupont, who is Mr. East's largest buyer, insists on clean titanium."

"Uh-huh. What's titanium? And how can you clean it? Sorry, Science isn't my best subject."

"Titanium is a metallic element found in sand and clay which is used in paint and face creams. Clean titanium means titanium mined with respect for the flora and fauna of the area and countryside."

"So how big is Mr. East's company?"

"Gigantic! It controls three of the largest sandmining areas in the world. Madagascar, Ukraine and the Murray-Darling Basin. And now they have gone into fracking for gas. My dad says it is going to contaminate the underground water."

Abba looked horrified. "And that is Damien's dad. No wonder he is scared. So what is this conference all about?"

"Mr. East, who is the managing director of the company, is trying to convince the government that his company won't wreck the Murray-Darling Basin."

"And why is your father here?

"To explain how the World Wildlife Fund checks out the mining sites and then makes suggestions as to what Mr. East's company can do to minimise destruction to the animals, birds, forests, sand dunes and sea."

"Does Mr. East's company listen to your dad?"

"Sometimes. But Dad says he's a hard nut to crack where big profits are concerned."

"He sounds awful."

"Awesomely awful if you ask me. On our way to Broome we saw him and Damien in Darwin. We were on the same Adelaide River crocodile cruise. Mr East was urging Damien to hang out over the boat to help feed the crocodiles. Damien wasn't having it, but his father kept telling him that if he wanted to succeed in life he had to challenge himself. Fortunately, my father doesn't think that way because I don't think I could have fed a chicken to a seven-metre-long crocodile. It took all my courage to lean over and get some good photographs."

"You were courageous last night."

Jimmy shrugged, as if that didn't count, even though he was pleased she'd said it. "I got the feeling from what Damien said yesterday that his father doesn't want him around much, and that he'd rather Damien lived with his mother." He spoke quickly so that she wouldn't notice how embarrassed her words had made him feel. "Which probably has to do with Damien being tossed out of two schools. Whereas the reason I'm here is because my dad wants us to have a man-to-man holiday together." He rolled his eyes to show what he thought of that, and she giggled.

"I think having a holiday with your father is cool," said Abba, studying her bare toes in her rubber flip flops. *Now he is going to ask me*, she thought. *Now it is my turn to confess all.*

"So, what does your father do?"

*Bingo!* She told her toes. Then she pushed back her hair and stared up at the cloudless blue sky while answering in a flat matter-of-fact voice. "He went back to Germany to see his family and never came back. Mum says his responsibilities over there must be greater than over here. But I reckon he just shot through and left us."

"So, you're half German."

"And quarter Aboriginal and quarter Indonesian, which is why I have curly black hair instead of straight black hair and Asian eyes."

Jimmy was considering how, without looking stupid, he could say that he liked the way she looked--that he liked her honey-brown skin and almond-shaped eyes--when Damien raced up looking like a model in a David Jones catalogue.

Jimmy swore silently. How many new pairs of labelled jeans, brand-new T-shirts and spotless white never-been-worn-before Reeboks did Damien with one 'm' own? And couldn't he have arrived five minutes later?

Damien frowned at them, clearly annoyed that they were there before him. "So, who are you two gossiping about?"

"Our fathers," said Abba.

Damien's handsome face relaxed a bit, "I was so close to being on the plane to London I could feel the wind under its wings. Fortunately, I didn't lie about watching videos because my dad had spoken to your dad. Did you get into trouble?"

Jimmy, still a bit annoyed at Damien's untimely arrival nodded coolly. "A bit. He was angry that I was late, and he was worried. But I reckon he was so relieved to see me that I only got half a lecture on how my mum would hit the roof if she knew I was gallivanting around Broome at midnight."

Damien grunted. "My mum couldn't care less."

Abba's mouth dropped open. "That's a terrible thing to say about your mum!"

Damien shrugged. "Maybe, but it's true. So is there any news about the floater?"

Abba shook her head. "Not in the newspaper or on TV. Either the police thought Jimmy's call was a joke or they're still looking for the body."

"I told them it was a white Toyota ute," insisted Jimmy.

"The ute might have been ditched and the murderers could have flown out this morning, or driven out last night," said Damien. "If I were them, I wouldn't be hanging around."

"Especially if I knew someone had a photograph of me. Which we will have by tomorrow morning," added Jimmy, already knowing the effect his words would have on the confident Damien, and feeling both mean and pleased about it at the same time.

Damien's heart began to beat faster. This morning his father had been as cold and as unresponsive as an iceberg. He wasn't even sure that his going to London wasn't still on the agenda. One more thing and he knew it would be.

Jimmy, seeing the look on Damien's face, grinned widely. "Relax Damien. I got the hotel office clerk to print them for me on her computer. She didn't even notice the photograph of torch-man running up the hill after us."

Damien flicked back his two matching waves of hair that hung over each ear and sighed dramatically. "I know you think I am paranoid but..."

"Only a little bit," grinned Jimmy.

"Enough," said Abba. "We have to pick up the broken bicycle and get it back to the hotel where my grandfather can mend it. You two have to come to help, because he is too old to heave a bike onto the back of a truck."

"What about you?" asked Damien.

"I'll be driving. He's too old to do that as well."

"Do you think we can get some photos of the rock ledge that has the stegosaurus footprint? I know it is underwater, but it would go well with my collection."

Abba raised her eyebrows. "It would just look like a photo of the seas."

"Him and his bloody camera," moaned Damien as Jimmy lopped off to fetch it. "If he hadn't taken a photograph of the torch man we wouldn't have been hunted by the men in the ute. Then we mightn't have been so late getting back."

"The torch man heard us talking," Abba reminded him. "It's just lucky we escaped."

"Lucky!" Damien shook his head at her. "I don't call shining his torch straight into your face lucky. If he comes from Broome, he might have recognised you. Just as he knows you might recognise him the minute you see his photograph. So he's not going to give up that easily. He's going to look for you and who you are; hanging out with such as a camera freak like Jimmy, and who he's hanging out with, such as me, and bingo he's got the three of us."

Abba's mouth formed a large 'O' and then she snapped it shut. "If you are trying to frighten me, Damien East, you are doing a brilliant job."

"Great! Because I think it is very possible that we are in a lot of danger. Wow! Who is that?"

"My grandfather."

Damien was astounded by Abba's grandfather.

Thomas Lou was a tiny, brown skinned, wrinkled-faced man wearing one green thong and one blue thong, a frayed pair of board shorts, a "Shark Ate MY Important Parts' T-shirt and an old straw hat that had seen better decades.

On reaching Damien and Abba, he greeted them like a teenager, slapping their hands in a high five salute while Abba grinned at Damien's surprised face. Five minutes later when Jimmy returned, he was greeted in the same noisy way.

Grandfather Lou, who talked nonstop, gave the boys the choice of sitting in the back of the truck, or squashed in the front seat with him and Abba. They chose the front seat as both wanted to see her drive. By the time they reached Gantheaume Point, Grandfather Lou had told them why the three *Matrix* films were his favourites, why he liked Jackie Chan's kung-fu films, rugby, soccer, Australian Rules Football and cricket, and why King Curly was his favourite rock group. "They are so cool," he crooned.

Jimmy and Damien were further amazed when Abba boasted that the old man had once been a pearl diver and a crocodile hunter and wrestler.

"Still do a bit of the old croc hunting but gave up the wrestling, those crocs are getting bigger every year," the old man added proudly. "Now I wrestle camels and sell pearls to tourists. You two need a pearl as a present for your mums?"

Damien and Jimmy shook their heads.

"What do you mean wrestle camels?" asked Jimmy.

"I take tourists on camel rides along Cable Beach. You come tonight and I give you a free ride."

Damien looked questioningly at Abba whose eyes were glued to the road as she drove carefully along it. He nudged her. "Will you be coming?"

"Depends. I have homework, and mum is angry about the broken bikes. If the hotel gardener notices them, she'll be in trouble."

"He won't," said Grandfather Lou. "So how about some music."

The truck pulled up at the beginning of the Lurujarri Walk with the four of them belting out "Mama Mia" Further up the track, past where they had left the broken bike there was a plastic police-strip blocking the way. Jimmy took a photograph of it.

Down on the rocks, police officers, people in normal clothes and a cluster of Aboriginal men were examining the area where the body had been. Further along the track a group of Aboriginal teenagers and women sat watching what was going on.

Minutes later, without anyone down on the rocks taking any notice, but with the Aborigines sitting on the track watching curiously, the three lifted the hotel bicycle into the back of the truck.

"So, what you want to do now?" asked Grandfather Lou.

Abba glanced at the boys, then answered for them. "If you could take the bike back to the hotel bike shed, we could see what's happening down there, then walk to Roebuck Bay and get the bus back."

"What about cleaning up the bicycle shed? That is your job you know, I not do it."

"I'll do it tomorrow."

"We'll help," added Jimmy.

"Fine with me," said the old man, tipping his hat over his eyes. "I got bait to get. I'm going barramundi fishing tomorrow."

"Why do you have to clean the bicycle shed?" asked Damien.

"It's my after-school job."

They watched Grandfather Lou back up the truck then they started off down the hill. A police office cut them off halfway.

"And where do you three think you are going?"

Abba smiled at him. "Hello, Constable Woodward. I wanted to show my friends something."

"What?"

"Some things down on the rocks."

"This is not a good time, Abba."

"We aren't going anywhere near where the police are," she wheedled. "We're going over there." She pointed to the stegosaur footprint pool where a lone policeman stood guard. "They're only here for a week. One of them is Mr. East's son. You know Mr. East; the sandmining man?"

The constable knew who Padric East was. All of Broome knew. There'd been a public meeting about the gas fracking and a double page write-up featuring a large photograph of Mr. East in the local paper. Most of the Broome residents were glad that there weren't any sand dunes worth mining in the Broome area and the rest were pleased that his company owned two Cable Beach hotels that brought in tourists to the town.

The constable shook his head. "You're too late."

"What do you mean, too late?" asked Damien.

"If it's the stegosaur footprints you're hoping to see. The ones that are hidden under the water at this time of day. The ones that no-one but the Aborigines are supposed to know about...which makes me wonder how you know about them, Abba. They're gone."

Abba's voice rose with shock. "What do you mean gone?"

"Gone! Disappeared! Cut or chipped out of the sandstone. Four perfect squares of rock picked up and stolen. Bob Cesar discovered the theft this morning while we were...looking for something else."

"And the tail indentation?" demanded Abba, "Is that gone too?"

The constable's eyebrows rose with surprise that there was such a thing. "I don't know anything about no tail thing. You'd have to ask Bob Cesar or one of the Aboriginal National Park guardians. Only now is not a good time because they are pretty angry. They have already sent for a curse-man. I reckon there will be a bit of bone pointing going on tonight. So if you want to watch you can sit on the track with the others, but you can't hang around here."

The boys followed Abba back up the hill. When they reached the spot opposite the rock pool where they'd hidden while the man with the torch looked for the floater, Abba pointed at the pool awash with transparent turquoise water.

"That's where the footprints were. That's why they were hammering and why they were wet. The tide was coming in over the prints when they were chipping them out. They weren't carrying a second body or even the first. They were carrying the footprints. I wish I'd known. I'd have bloody-well tripped them up."

Damien stared down at the pretty pool. "Who would want to steal four sandstone footprints?"

"Fossil poachers," answered Jimmy. "Dinosaur fossils are a multimillion-dollar business."

"You're having me on," scoffed Damien.

"No, I'm not," snapped Jimmy, who was annoyed at having his word questioned by someone who probably only knew the price of his Calvin Klein socks, and precious little else.

"Don't you know anything? For your information, there are fifty fossil collectors in Australia who spend over fifty thousand dollars a year each on acquiring fossils."

"And the skeleton of a Tyrannosaurus Rex, commonly known as the tyrant lizard king, sold for eight million USA dollars last year," added Abba.

Damien looked down at the pool again and then along the rocky shore at the red pindan cliffs of Reddell Beach. "Are there any more stegosaurus footprints?"

"Thousands," said Abba, staring out over the cliffs, imagining them scattered with herds of dinosaurs of all sizes browsing on the marshy lagoon grass that used to grow there, with one or two meat-eating tetrapods watching, waiting to attack.

Then she sighed. "But the stolen ones were the only matching four so far discovered hereabouts. That's why they are unique and worth a fortune I bet."

"So why weren't they guarded?"

"Because guarding them would cost a fortune. Because they were hidden under the water most of the time. Because Broome is so remote," she threw up her hands. "How do I know!"

"So how much will they be worth?"

Abba glanced at Jimmy, who rolled his eyes skywards as he calculated. "Two five-digit front feet and two three-toed back feet about 120 million years old, from Australia where the stegosaurus are not common would bring about ....one million USA dollars. More if they've taken the tall indentation. It would make a perfect set. The five bits set up as if a stegosaurus was walking along would look fantastic. Especially if there was a plastic model of a stegosaur or skeleton suspended above the footprints and a sound recording of imaginary dinosaur noises coming from somewhere close."

Damien stared at him. "You really like this dinosaur stuff, don't you?"

"Yes. When I finish high school, I'm going to go to university to become a palaeontologist."

"Me too," added Abba, "If I can afford to go to university, that is."

Damien looked at the both of them as if seeing them for the first time. A stocky blond-haired boy with determined grey eyes and a slim dark-skinned girl with up-tilted black eyes. Both knowing exactly what they wanted to do when they finished school. He was impressed, especially as he didn't have a clue what he was going to do, only what he didn't want to do. He didn't want to be a businessman. A fact that upset his father daily.

"So, who would pay that much for four bits of stone?'

Abba began walking along the track. "Overseas museums or private collectors. It's rumoured that a well-known prince has a fossil wish list, so he might pay a million."

Damien frowned at the back of her faded T-shirt. "What's a fossil wish list?"

"It's a list of fossils wanted by collectors which is circulated, supposedly in search of the item, but really for fossil poachers to know what to steal," explained Jimmy. "Do you remember the Psittacosaurus skeleton that was stolen from Newcastle Museum a few years back?"

Damien shook his head. "Sitta.... What?"

"*Psittaco* meaning parrot-beaked *saurus* meaning lizard. The skeleton that was stolen belonged to China and it was on loan."

Damien shook his head again. "Never heard of it."

"Well, it was probably on a collector's wish list and the thief simply followed the exhibition around until he saw an opportunity to steal it."

"But how would you steal a skeleton? Wouldn't it fall apart?"

"No. It would be wired together, and you would have to be careful and have a padded suitcase to put it in. Stealing the stego footprints was a lot easier if heavier."

Abba spun round to face them. "Which is why we have to send the photograph of the torch man to the police with an anonymous note saying what we saw."

"No way!" cried Damien. "Police can check hand-writing. They would know who sent the note. And they can easily trace who printed off the photographs. I'd be on a plane to London faster than yesterday."

"We could write the letter by sticking bits of the newspaper together," said Abba.

"They can check the sweat from your fingers on the newspaper."

"I'll wear plastic gloves. And I'll say it was only Jimmy and me who saw the murder," argued Abba.

"Do you think my father is stupid? He'd put two and two together and know why we were late last night."

"My dad wouldn't be too impressed either," added Jimmy. "I promised him that going to photograph the footprints it would be as safe as going to the cinema."

"We have to do something," replied Abba sharply. "When I found the footprints, I thought I was the only one who knew about them. I've been hiding them under seaweed for years. Now they've been stolen, and I feel responsible. I want them back."

Jimmy caught up with her. "They are probably out of Australia by now. Fossil poachers get the item to the fossil broker as fast as they can. They don't hang around."

Damien stared at the two of them in frustration. "Will you both speak English! What is a fossil broker?"

"A fossil broker is the person who will sell the stolen fossil for the thieves."

"Sssshhh," Abba gestured to the group further up the track. "They'll hear you."

"How's it going cuz?" shouted one of the Aboriginal women.

"Not so good," Abba shouted back. "I just heard the news."

"Bad news, eh?"

Abba nodded, then she spoke to the boys. "I'll be back in a minute. I'm off to have a chat with my aunty."

The boys watched her walk over to the women, slap a few hands, then hunker down beside them and begin talking.

"Do you think that woman really is her aunty?" said Damien.

Jimmy glanced at the dark-skinned, bare-footed woman in the floral dress. "I think all that is needed to be an aunty is to be related in some way, or come from the same part of the country, or the same mob."

Damien picked a piece of grass and waved it in front of his face to keep the flies away. "So, what's the chances of finding these footprints?"

Jimmy made a face. "None. The next time they surface it'll be at a fossil and mineral trade fair in Denver or Hamburg. That's what happens to the fossils smuggled out of China, Ukraine and Canada. You can even buy snuggled dino eggs off the internet."

"People buy dino eggs?"

"Sure. Just last month a tarbosaurus egg sold for three thousand USA dollars. That's because a tarbosaurus is first cousin to the Tyrannosaurus

Rex and because the egg is about..." Jimmy stretched out his arm and measured from his elbow to the tip of his fingers, "This long. Most eggs, such as those of the duck-billed hadrosaur, are as big as grapefruits. They fetch about two hundred and fifty USA dollars, unless they're in a cluster of eggs. Clusters cost more even if they have no identity papers."

Damien looked surprised. "Dinosaur eggs have identity papers?"

"All legal fossils have identity papers. It's like a birth certificate. But not having them won't stop Abba's stego footprints from being sold. The buyers will know they've been stolen because the Australian Government doesn't allow fossils to be taken out of the country."

Damien brushed more flies away. "So how come you and Abba know so much about this sort of thing?"

Jimmy smiled broadly. "We're fossil freaks. That's how I met Abba. I went on the internet to see if there were any fossil freaks in Broome and she answered. When I arrived and we got talking she offered to show me the footprints as long as I told no-one, and I promised to send her photographs of my fossils. Then you came along and promised you wouldn't tell anyone."

Damien flicked a large fluttering insect off his T-shirt sleeve. "Which was no big deal, as I know zilch about dinosaur footprints."

"Well, now you do. Which reminds me. I could be the only person on earth that has photographed those footprints."

Damien gave up on brushing insects off his clothes and out of his eyes and pulled his T-shirt over his head so that his face was covered. "So, what good will it do you?" he asked.

Jimmy waved his piece of grass faster in front of his freckled nose. "I could put them on eBay to sell. I could put them on Facebook to warn legitimate dealers that they've been stolen. I could offer the photographs to the Australian museum which might put up a reward for the footprints return. I could use them to check against other stegosaurus footprint photographs that might be for sale on the internet."

"What might be for sale?" asked Abba, sitting down beside them.

"My stegosaurus footprint photos. What did your aunty say?"

"That the police have sent for an anthropologist and a palaeontologist who are both on their way from Perth. The man in khaki is a Native Title Claims officer. The Aboriginal in the red shirt is one of the Roe family, who are the custodians of this sacred site. They are very upset at the site being desecrated and that the soul-line of a Dreaming creature has been broken. By Aboriginal law that's a crime punishable by death. So, they've sent for a curse-man to put curses on the thieves."

"You don't believe in curse-men, do you?" scoffed Damien.

"Oh yes I do. In 1998 a theropod footprint and a rare human footprint were stolen from around here. They were never recovered but one of the thieves was caught. He's in jail and he's been sick from the day they put him there. His brother who everyone thinks was involved, died soon after the robbery. So I want the fossil poachers caught and the footprints put back, before we start getting sick. Especially Jimmy, as he took the photographs. They're probably cursed as well."

Damien elbowed Jimmy in the ribs. "How do you feel? Feeling sick? Want to chuck up? Or do you need a body around for that?"

Jimmy kicked Damien's brand-new Reeboks. "Shut up, big mouth. If I get sick then you get sick, just remember that."

Abba slapped both of them on their arms to get their attention. "The Aboriginal man in the blue shirt is Bob Cesar from the Bardi people. He's a tracker who reads footprints better than we read books. He'll know how many people were on the rocks. He might even find our tracks, especially where Damien and I crawled all over the place. So, I reckon we've hung around the crime scene long enough."

As they passed the Aboriginal group, Abba called goodbye, and someone shouted back. "On ya, cuz."

"So, what reason did you give your aunty for us being here?" asked Jimmy.

"I told them we were riding our bikes along the track yesterday afternoon when we buckled a wheel. Bob Cesar will find the tyre marks anyway. The only problem is, he'll probably know it wasn't yesterday afternoon."

"How will he know?" demanded Damien.

"From the night insects and night animals that will have walked over the tyre tracks and the night insects that we squashed by the bikes."

Damien scuffed at the sand. "So, what do we say if we are asked why we were out so late?"

"It mightn't happen," Abba assured him, but deep down she was afraid it would. It was rumoured that Bob Cesar could almost smell where a person had walked.

They were hot and thirsty by the time they reached Port Drive.

"I need a drink," gasped Damien, heading for the shade of the bus shelter. "Any shops around?"

"We could walk down to Roebuck Bay, and I could show you where nine Japanese planes blew up sixteen flying boats and killed a hundred and forty people," Abba answered without much enthusiasm. "Or...we could catch the bus back to the hotel."

Jimmy collapsed beside Damien. "What do you want to do?"

"Well, I have hardly seen my mum all week because she's been working nights at the hotel. She'll be awake by now, so I'd like to catch the bus and get off at my house while you two go to the hotel."

Damien stretched his long legs and yawned. "Suits me. I want to go for a swim. So why did the Japanese blow up the flying boats?"

Abba rested her head back against the shelter wall and closed her eyes; she hadn't slept well on the hotel sofa, and she was tired. "It was during the Second World War. The Japanese air force was angry that the Dutch were escaping from the Dutch East Indies, so they bombed them."

"Didn't the Australians try to shoot down the Japanese planes?"

"There were no anti-aircraft guns, because Broome was supposed to be outside of Japanese flying range; only the Japanese had developed long range fuel tanks. But a machine gun on one of the refugee flying boats shot down a Japanese plane."

"What about all the Japanese pearlers who were living here?" asked Jimmy.

"A lot had gone back to Japan. The rest were in detention camps. Which was crazy, as the Japanese pearlers didn't care about the war. And without them the pearling industry couldn't work, and without the pearling industry Broome went broke."

"You know," said Damien, staring over the road at a row of dark green mango trees. "There's a lot more to Broome than you first think. There are stegosaurs' footprints. Japanese pearlers, bombed flying boats, fossil poachers. This holiday is more exciting than I expected it to be."

"We aim to please, said Abba, tiredly. Then she perked up as she saw the bus coming. "When I'm not so tired, remind me to tell you about the battle between the Japanese Pearlers and the Malay pearlers. That was really something."

Abba was to leave the bus before the boys. As it rounded a corner on the edge of town, she pointed out a two-storied wooden house set back in a grove of coconut palms and surrounded by a fence so overloaded with red and white bougainvillea that it had collapsed in places. There was no gate only a long-overgrown driveway.

"That's our house," she said proudly, as she pressed the bus's stop button. "My grandfather built it for my grandmother. It was the first house she'd ever lived in and the first Asian house allowed on the white people's side of the train track. What time will you get the photos, Jimmy?"

"In the morning."

"So, I'll see you after breakfast. I'll be cleaning out the bike shed." Then with a wave and a flick of the fringe of her sarong, she swung down the steps onto the grass verge and was away running along the footpath until she disappeared into the driveway.

"It looks pretty lonely," said Damien. "I mean sort of spooky with all those trees around it."

Jimmy was agreeing when his eyes widened, and he twisted round in his seat. "Did you see that?"

"What?"

"A white ute parked down that side street behind Abba's house."

"Did you see its number plate?"

Jimmy leant back against the bus seat. "Nah. But it was a Toyota. What if it's the torch man? What if he's waiting for Abba? Shouldn't we get off at the next stop and warn her?"

Damien shook his head. "Her grandfather and her mother are there, so nothing is going to happen to her; and there are probably a hundred white utes in Broome. It's sort of a white ute town."

Jimmy had to agree that it was, but he was still worried.

They alighted from the bus at Cable Beach just as the sun was setting into the Indian Ocean and the sky was streaked with gold and scarlet. The red reminded Jimmy of the slick of blood the floater had left on the rock.

Damien leant on the fence that overlooked the beach. Below them bathers were still splashing around in the warm sea. Others sat on the sand watching the volcanic-looking sky, while still others balanced upon a string of camels swaying away into the lavender-coloured night. "Do you know, if you kept swimming west, you'd bump into Zanzibar."

"Or Africa and the Rift Valley and you could find some of the oldest fossils in the world," answered Jimmy dreamily, then he noticed the camels.

"Oh no! Abba's grandfather isn't going to be at home tonight. He's taking the tourist on a camel trek. Remember how he offered for us to go free?"

Damien looked a bit worried. "But her mother will be there."

Jimmy shrugged. "How do we know that? I think we should ring and tell Abba about the ute."

"How? My mobile is back at the hotel."

"And I don't have one," finished Jimmy, looking around for a public phone box, which seemed unlikely this close to the beach.

"And she didn't give us her phone number," finished Damien.

"We can get it from the hotel receptionist," shouted Jimmy, beginning to run.

The Broome Sunmoon Hotel was considered one of the best hotels in Broome. Its gardens were spectacular. Its entrance, which brought excited oohs and aaahs from arriving tourists, was reached by crossing a red Japanese-style bridge straddling a fishpond full of goldfish and shiny white pebbles. Inside the marble-floored reception area which was flanked with stone Chinese lions and tall Xian terracotta warriors was especially imposing.

"Not very Broome like," scoffed Damien, who was used to expensive hotels. "Let me do the speaking."

He strode up to the smiling receptionist's counter. "I wonder if you could help me?"

But the receptionist was unwilling to give him Abba's mother's phone number or any information as to whether Abba's mother was working tonight or not.

"I don't think she would like it," she added, smiling at them as if she'd just told them they'd won the lottery.

"This is a life-and-death situation," insisted Damien.

She continued to smile like a toothpaste advertisement. "They always are."

"How about you give us Abba's surname and we'll look it up in the phone book," insisted Damien.

More smiles. "If you are such good friends, you'd know her surname."

"Then all you have to do is say yes or no as to whether her mother is working tonight. Or do I have to ask my father, Padric West, to find out for me?"

The receptionist's smile disappeared, and her eyes narrowed as she answered him in a cool, wish-I-could-string-you-up-by-your thumbs voice. "Abba's mother is working tonight. But I happen to know that she is very strict with Abba and boys. Do you want to talk to her?"

Just then Jimmy's father walked into the hotel foyer. "Jimmy! Hello Damien! I've been looking everywhere for you, Jimmy. Where have you been?"

As Jimmy looked tongue tied, Damien answered for him. "We've been watching the sunset at Cable Beach. It was amazing, Mr Chadwick."

"All afternoon?" queried Paul Chadwick. "Then you must have seen the ghost of Dampier's ship."

Both boys looked puzzled.

"Are you having us on?" said Jimmy.

"Never. Dampier was supposed to have buried his treasure along this coast. The locals say that his ghost ship sails up and down looking for it.

They believe it so much that people go treasure hunting and blow up the sand dunes looking for it. I'm doing research on it for the World Wildlife Fund this very moment."

Jimmy glanced at Damien and grinned. "There's a lot more to Broome than..."

"Are you coming to dinner?" interrupted his father. "Because I've some people to speak to afterwards and I want to get moving."

Jimmy thought quickly. "Can I go to McDonalds with Damien? I'm a bit sick of hotel food and Maccas has a bargain night on."

"Then we thought we'd go to the outdoor Sun Picture theatre," added Damien.

Paul Chadwick regarded the boys with a knowing eye. They were up to something; but then, when weren't boys up to something? But he was glad to see that they'd made friends since there was no-one else of Jimmy's age at the conference. He hadn't thought they would hit it off, they were so different. Damien with his fashionable labelled clothes, sophisticated beyond his years manner, and if his father's complaining was right, a bit of a problem at school, and nerdy, bookish Jimmy with his sticking up hair and serious grey eyes wearing last year's shorts and shirts. They made an unlikely pair that was for sure, but so what if they stuffed themselves silly with junk food for one night. It couldn't hurt this once.

"Sun Pictures. Isn't that the old Chinese cinema where you sit in canvas chairs?"

Jimmy nodded.

"Then I can't see why not, but no more late nights. I want you back by ten. I promised your mother you'd ring her early tomorrow morning."

"Done," shouted Jimmy. "See ya." He was halfway across the foyer when he remembered his father's speech, "Dad! How did your speech go?"

"Very well. I'll tell you about it when you get back."

"The bike shed," yelled Damien the minute they were outside the hotel.

Jimmy raced after him. "How will we find the house?"

"Follow the bus route."

# Chapter 4

A bba read the note she found on the kitchen table. 'Hotel needs me to work. Back midnight. Dinner in fridge, love and hugs and kisses, Mum.'

Abba opened the fridge. Ignoring the silver-foil covered plate she took out the bread, butter, peanut butter, golden syrup, pickles and cheese and began to make a mega sandwich.

It didn't bother her being in the house alone. She'd lived here all her life and knew every corner. Every creak of its veranda timbers and its polished wooden floors, every rattle of its tin roof and guttering. She loved its oldness. Especially the three-generation-old teak furniture from Indonesia with the cushions her mother covered with cast-off bedspreads from the hotel, and the old photographs of the pearling luggers her grandfather and great grandfather had worked on. It would be her house one day, and she was glad, because she loved it. But tonight, it did feel a bit strange.

It wasn't because her grandfather was out walking his camels and wouldn't be back until ten after he'd had a few beers with his mates. And it wasn't because her mother was working late. Her mother only had two nights off work a week. It was more a sort of spooky feeling that wouldn't go away like a menacing evil weight on her shoulders, or a creepy wind blowing around the house as if something bad was coming to get it.

"It's the desert wind," she told the kitchen bench. "It feels like it's winding up to become a cyclone, only it isn't cyclone season."

Talking to whichever room she was in was a habit of Abba's. It usually made her feel better. This time with the breeze stirring the papers stuck on the fridge and the wind disturbing the bougainvillea at the window and rattling the palms in the garden, talking to the kitchen bench didn't work. She felt very, very alone.

"Like the only person on the planet," she told the staircase as she climbed it to her bedroom, "No, like the only person in the universe."

She switched on her bedroom light. "It's the curse of the stolen stegosaurus footprint," she joked as she switched on her computer. "It wasn't me," she told the room as she slipped a CD into her player. "But I am going to find out who it was."

As the group *Abba*'s hit *'Does your mother know you're out'*, filled her bedroom, Abba clicked on the Net, typed in dinosaurs, pressed search, and up came a worldwide list of dinosaur fossil traders. Another click and pages of advertisements came up. They were selling beautiful, preserved Jurassic vertebras, late Cretaceous ankle bones, a baby titanosaurid's skull smaller than her hand, several seventy-million-year- old Patagonian embryos, a cluster of tarbosaurus and sauropod eggs the size of cannon balls, and thousands of Mongolian dendroolithus dinosaur eggs.

It was so interesting that she lost time and was deep in the Net hunting for dinosaur footprints when she heard the first unusual creak.

It came from the veranda below her room. The nightingale veranda her grandfather called it, after a famous squeaking veranda in the Imperial Kyoto Palace in Japan.

"It squeaked every time someone walked on it, which warned the Shogun of Kyoto that an assassin was coming to get him," he'd explained.

"An assassin is coming to get me," she jokingly told her screen. Then she heard a second squeak, and she stopped joking.

She was wondering if she should turn the music off so she could hear better, or whether that might warn the prowler that she'd heard something, when she heard the third creak. It was closer.

Funny how noises made from the wind or old wood dying after rain sounded different to the squeak of someone creeping around a veranda.

She quietly pushed back her chair and tiptoed to her window. There was no-one outside on her veranda, and unless she went out onto it she wouldn't be able to look over the railing to see if there was anyone on the veranda below. *And I am not doing that*, she decided. *What I am going to do is go downstairs to make sure the back door and the front door is locked.*

Her floorboards creaked, the upstairs passageway's floor creaked and the stairs creaked, even though she avoided walking in the middle of them. She hoped the creaks didn't sound as loud to whoever was outside as they did to her. The thought whoever was outside hung in the air in front of her as she tiptoed along the ground floor passage.

*You're being silly,* she chided herself. *It's only next door's dog padding around waiting for you to throw him something to eat. Or a stray cat.* But she dismissed that idea. Cats never made floors creak. It was as if all the cats in the world had an agreement with all the floors in the world that there'd be no creaking. She bet a cat could walk over the Kyoto palace nightingale floor without a sound.

Which leaves the curse-man, she decided as she pushed the old-fashioned bolt across the front door.

Abba believed implicitly in the curse-man. Her grandmother, and elder of the Rubiki tribe, had told her all about him. "He creeps around in his emu-feathered shoes so you can't hear him weaving a string of curse-grass around you. Then when you step over the curse-grass string, or you break it you get sick and die."

Was the curse-man weaving a string of curse-grass around her house because she knew about the stolen dinosaur footprints?

She turned towards the back door and was creeping past the staircase thinking how stupid she was being, when all the lights in the house went off. Upstairs Frieda of Abba stopped singing '*Fernando*'.

Abba held her breath. She couldn't hear a thing except the rattle of the palm fronds smashing against each other. But she knew that for the lights to go off someone had to turn them off at the main switch box in the kitchen.

Swinging round, she raced back towards the bolted front door. Reaching the staircase, she thought about galloping up it but then she remembered her grandmother telling her that panicking humans and primates always climbed up when they wanted to escape but that it wasn't always the best thing to do, so she raced on into the darkness with her arms outstretched and her fingers spread wide so that she wouldn't bump into the hatstand.

She had passed it when the man grabbed her around the waist and threw her backwards.

Her head hit the hatstand and she went sprawling along the polished wooden floor as the hatstand crashed down behind her. In an instant she was up and running. She heard the man swear as the hatstand was kicked out of the way.

She reached the kitchen and was fighting with the kitchen doorknob when he caught her again. This time he gripped her around the neck with one hand while he pulled a plastic onion sack over her head and shoulders with the other. Next, he pulled her hands behind her back and bound them with cord, then he dragged her, kicking and screaming through the onion bag weave towards the lounge room. Here he pushed her into one of the cared chairs, slapped her across the head and threatened to knock her block off if she didn't shut up.

She gulped back a scream as he clamped his hand over her mouth.

"Where's the camera? Where's the film? Where are the photos?" He hissed. Then he removed his hand so she could answer.

"The camera smashed on the rocks and fell into the sea when we were running away."

"Liar!" He shook her hard and banged her head against the back of the chair. "Who's got the camera?"

"No one! It's at the bottom of the sea."

"Who are the two boys who were with you?"

"Tourists. They went back to Sydney today on the morning plane."

"Liar!" His face was so close that she could feel his hot breath through the onion bag. "Now you listen to me, if you tell anyone what you saw or you show anyone those photos, I'll get you, your mum and your crazy old grandfather. And I can do it because I have powerful friends in the right places, so make no mistake missy, you are mixing yourself up in a very dangerous business. Do you understand?"

Abba was nodding and trying not to cry when she heard banging on the front door followed by loud voices yelling her name.

"Abba! Abba! Are you all right? We've called the police and they're on their way. Are you there?"

"Help!" she yelled back.

A split second later the chair was pushed backwards, and she was flying through the air.

Jimmy and Damien heard the bang as the chair hit the wooden floor.

"Back door," shouted Jimmy sprinting around the veranda. But that side of the house was blocked off by a prickly bougainvillea bush.

"Other way!" he shouted.

When they reached the back door, it was swinging open. The house was in darkness and from somewhere inside Abba was shouting.

"Light switch," yelled Damien feeling for the switch. He found it inside the door, but it didn't work. "Someone's turned off the lights, we'll have to feel our way."

Jimmy hesitated. "What if the attackers are still in there?"

"There's two of us. Find a weapon."

Jimmy found the broom behind the door and Damien picked up the bread knife that Abba had used to make her sandwich.

They were feeling their way along the passageway when they heard the sound of a car revving up and then taking off at top speed.

"I think that was the ute," said Jimmy stepping forward with more confidence and tripping over the hatstand. With a yell he fell onto a pile of hats and jackets with Damien teetering close behind.

"Jimmy! Damien!" shouted Abba. "I'm tied up!"

"Where are you?" yelled Damien.

"In the lounge room."

The lounge room wasn't as dark as the rest of the house because of the moon shining through the French doors. Abba was standing near a cared sofa.

Jimmy raced across the room and pulled the onion bag off her head. As it came off her wide frightened eyes glanced around the room. "Has he gone?"

"Think so. We heard the sound of an engine."

"It was the torch-man. He wanted to know where the camera and film were and who you two were. I told him you'd caught the morning plane and..." She stopped for a breath. "He said if I told anyone what we'd seen, he'd get my mum and my grandfather and us. He said he was involved with some very dangerous people. I think he was threatening to kill us."

"But he didn't, and he won't," said Damien patting her awkwardly on the shoulder.

"How do you know?" demanded Jimmy, who was not liking the way Damien had taken charge.

"He didn't kill the man in the sea, it was the white head man. So I reckon torch man was after the camera to get rid of the evidence proving that he was there. He wanted to frighten Abba, not kill her. Otherwise, he would have done it already. It would have been the best way to shut her up. Right?"

"It didn't feel like he was just trying to frighten me when I had a sack over my head," muttered Abba. "And will someone please undo my hands. And where are the police?"

"We lied," said Jimmy as he undid the cord. "But we can call them now."

"And say what?" asked Damien. "That one of the men we saw murder someone while they were stealing stegosaur footprints in a National Park that we weren't supposed to be in, attacked Abba because we have an incriminating photograph that we have not shown to the police. What do you think our parents will say when we are arrested for obstructing justice? I'll tell you what they will say. My dad will send me to London never to set foot on Australian soil again. That's if we aren't sent to a correctional centre for breaking the law. So what will your father do Jimmy?"

"I reckon he'd ground me for life. What will your mother do, Abba?"

"She'd blame herself because she works nights and she would leave her job which she has worked so hard to get and which she loves, and we'd be broke again and it would all be my fault."

"So, here is the alternative," said Damien. "We wait to see what the photographs look like. If Abba recognises the torch-man, then we'll let him know that we know who he is and that we will keep quiet if he leaves Abba alone. He won't know we are only staying quiet until we find out who the murderer is. Once we find that out we hand everything over to the police. And we'll be famous. There might even be a reward for saving the footprints."

Jimmy agreed that Damien' plan was pretty good. He especially liked the famous part, but considering what had happened to Abba threatening the torch man or even trying to make a bargain with him could be dangerous. "So, I reckon, as a backup we send the photographs anonymously to the police and leave it up to them."

"But it wouldn't be anonymous," insisted Damien. "Torch-man would want to use us as witnesses to prove that he didn't kill anyone. The police would be here looking for us at Abba's house five minutes after they picked him up and he squealed. What do you think, Abba?"

"I think we should turn the lights on and clean up the hatstand mess. By then I might have come up with a better idea than both of yours."

They felt their way back to the kitchen to the main electricity box and switched on the lights. In the bright kitchen Abba's bruises were beginning to show.

Jimmy winced at the sight of Abba's face. "You're going to have a black eye."

"And a bruised hip," she added. "Does anyone feel like eating? I make a terrific sandwich, and suddenly I am starving."

After their monster sandwiches Jimmy told Abba how once they'd realised she was home alone they'd tried to get her phone number to warn her about seeing the white ute hanging around.

"Then we grabbed the bikes and followed the bus route back to here so we wouldn't get lost," continued Damien.

"Who's getting lost?" asked Grandfather Lou walking into the kitchen. "And do you two know how late it is?"

Damien looked at his watch. "Oh no! It's after ten. We have to go."

"Same place same time," Jimmy yelled at Abba as he raced after Damien.

"Wouldn't miss it for quids," yelled Abba.

They were riding out of her gate when she caught up with them. "Don't show the photographs to Damien first. Let's look at them all together. Promise?"

"Promise!" shouted Jimmy.

They pedalled as fast as they could, but Jimmy was still half an hour late when he raced, red-faced and sweaty, into the hotel room.

His father smiled to himself and pretended not to notice the time.

"So," said Jimmy after he'd showered and was lying on the twin bed opposite his father. "How did the conference go, Dad? Are you winning the battle against the big bad global giants?"

Paul Chadwick considered his son's flippant question, then he answered it seriously. "If you mean have I shown that World Wide Fund cannot be trifled with, then yes I am winning."

"How'd Mr West take that?"

"Without enthusiasm. It costs more money to look after the environment when sandmining. How are you getting on with his son?"

"Damien! He's okay. A bit bossy but okay."

In fact, thought Jimmy as he rolled over and buried his head in his pillow, Damien spelt with one 'm' was more than okay. He was cool. If only he wasn't so scared of being shipped off to London. Because whether Damien liked it or not, they had witnessed a crime and eventually they'd have to own up to someone if only to help identify the murderers.

"So how are you getting on with Jimmy Chadwick?" called Damien's father from his bedroom. "Is he too young for you? Or do you think you'll keep in touch after we leave Broome?"

Damien rubbed his hair dry then slipped on the hotel's towelling dressing gown. "He's only half a year younger and he's pretty interesting. He knows all about dinosaurs and fossils. For instance, did you know there is a new dinosaur discovered every seven weeks? Jimmy does. He's going to be a palaeontologist when he grows up."

"And what are you going to be, Damien?"

Damien made a face at himself in the bathroom mirror. He had left himself wide open for that one. "I haven't decided yet," he called, already knowing his father's response.

"Surprise. Surprise," muttered his father, loud enough for Damien to hear.

Damien looked at his reflection in the mirror and mouthed his father's words at himself. *Surprise, surprise.* Then he smiled. His father had no idea what was going on.

# Chapter 5

Abba had the bikes out and the shed swept by the time the boys arrived.

Damien grinned at her. "I like your black eye."

"You should see the rest of me," joked Abba.

"What did your grandfather and mother say about your bruises?" asked Jimmy.

"If I had told them there was a man in the house Grandfather Lou would have sat up all night with his kangaroo gun and Mum would never work night shift again. So I told them I was running through the house and fell over the hatstand. Which is sort of true."

Damien nodded, he was a master at telling half-truths, it was the way he survived living with his dad. "So, what are you doing now?"

"I've got ten bikes to clean. Want to help?"

"Not much," answered Damien before Jimmy could answer. "I was planning on hitting the pool. Want to come?"

Abba shook her head. "The pool is for guests only. But if you don't want to help me then I won't tell you my fantastic news and my fantastic idea of getting us out of this mess."

"What mess?" grinned Damien. "Jimmy and I are out of here in two days. We ain't got no mess, bro."

Abba put her hands on her hips and tilted her head. "Then you are going to have a big mess, bro, if you don't help me clean these bikes because you are going to wear this." She swooped down and picked up a bucket of soapy water and walked towards him.

"What do we have to do?" laughed Jimmy as the water sloshed over Damien's new Reeboks.

"Check the tyres, brakes and seats then wipe each bike with a damp cloth."

Jimmy threw Damien a cloth. "You wipe, I'll check. So, what's your fantastic news, Abba?"

"They found the body yesterday. Only the police kept it a secret while Bob Cesar did his tracking. The body is Albert Thon. He used to own a souvenir and shell shop in China Town. He was a real slimy character and was suspected of stealing shell from the pearl reefs north of town. Grandpa told me."

"Did the police mention the stolen stegosaur footprints?"

"Not a word. I think they are waiting for the palaeontologist from Perth to arrive. But there is more."

"Go on," urged Jimmy.

"You're going to like this bit. They're looking for six people. Three adults and three teenagers, or two teenagers and a twelve-year-old child...those are probably my little feet."

"Oh hell!" exclaimed Damien, throwing his cloth into the bucket and accidentally splashing Jimmy.

"Watch it!" Exclaimed Jimmy, then to Abba, "So what's your plan?"

"Show me the photos first. Did you show them to Damien?"

Jimmy handed her the photos. "No, although he nagged me all through breakfast. Even offered to bribe me with his scrambled eggs."

Abba patted his blond hair. "Good lad," she said putting on her mother's voice. Then she opened the envelope and sifted through the photographs. "Great ones of the footprints. Oh!" she held up two of the torch-man. "I know him. His name is Sammy Jacob, and he lives near Willie Creek and works at the Willie Creek Pearl Farm. My grandfather buys bait from him and sometimes they fish together...Oh no!"

"Oh no what?" demanded Damien.

"It just occurred to me that....no surely he wouldn't. I swore him to secrecy the day I found them."

"Found what? Who to secrecy?" shouted Jimmy and Damien together.

"Remember how I said I'd only told two people about the footprints...my grandfather and you, Jimmy. What if my grandfather told Sammy Jacob. I can't imagine he would but...if he did it would be my fault that the footprints were stolen. It would be my fault that Albert Thon was murdered."

Jimmy rolled his eyes at Damien, "No it wouldn't. It's the fault of the thieves and the man with the white hair and the hammer."

"But..."

"No buts. Look at the rest of the photos."

Abba held out a third photo of Sammy Jacob behind him was the man with the hammer.

"Who is that?" asked Damien.

"Don't know." Abba checked the next two photographs; each was an enlargement of the two men's faces.

"When I asked the World Wildlife Fund to get enlargements of any faces, I didn't know about the man with the white hair being in them. He must have come up after Sammy Jacobs shouted that he had seen us."

Abba stared hard at the white-haired man. "He isn't from Broome."

"I thought we could go round the hotels and ask the receptionists if he's been staying at their hotel," said Jimmy. "But first tell us your fantastic plan."

Abba put the photos down on an upturned bucket. "It's not so fantastic now. I was hoping I'd recognise the torch-man and that we could telephone him and tell him that if he went to the police, we'd be witnesses to say he didn't hit Albert Thon. That way the police would catch the murderer and find the stegosaur footprints. We'd be heroes and Damien's father wouldn't be mad at him anymore. Only...we can't do that now."

Jimmy picked up the photographs. "Why not?"

"Because Sammy doesn't have a phone in his fishing shack, which means we would have to tell him face to face; and I'm not so keen on doing that."

"And even if we did, what makes you think he would go to the police instead of sticking an onion bag over all our heads?" said Damien.

"Because we have his photograph," Jimmy answered for Abba, "which we can threaten to send to the police if he hurts us or Abba."

"Does your camera date and time each photograph?"

"No. It's an old camera."

"Then he can say that the photos were taken another day. It would be our word against his. So, I ask again. Why would he dob himself in?"

"Because if he didn't," said Abba. "I was going to threaten to tell the curse-man about him. Sammy's from Broome. He knows how powerful a curse-man can be."

"What is a curse-man?" asked Jimmy.

"An Aboriginal elder."

"I don't believe an Aboriginal elder will make Sammy dob himself in," muttered Damien.

Abba glared at him. "You don't know everything Damien West, even if you think you do. And you're not wiping that bike properly."

"What if Sammy does a runner?" asked Jimmy trying to change the subject.

Abba shook her head. "He won't. He knows that a curse-man will find him no matter where he goes. Curse-men have been known to search through time and all four states."

"You're suggesting that we go to Willie Creek Pearl Farm and confront this Sammy and threaten him with the curse-man. Is that your plan?" said Damien.

Abba nodded, then shook her head, and then dropped her head into her hands. "Not we. You two. I can't afford the tour bus to Willie Creek, and I promised my mum I'd help clean our house this afternoon and..." her voice dropped to a dramatic whisper. "I don't want to see Sammy Jacobs ever again. I don't want to go near him. I hate him for frightening me that much."

"I hate him too," announced Damien, in exactly the same low dramatic voice she had used.

Abba looked up quickly.

"Well, I would," he continued, grinning at her, "If I'd let him put a sack over my head and let him throw me at the hatstand."

"I didn't let him!" she yelled throwing her wet cloth at him.

The cloth went sailing past Damien and hit Jimmy.

Jimmy picked it up and threw it at Damien. It hit him square in the chest.

"Watch it! That's a clean shirt!"

"Oooooh! My clean shirt," imitated Abba.

"What if Sammy beats us both up?" shouted Jimmy over the both of them.

"He won't," said Abba. "Not if you keep your distance. And the minute I've finished helping my mum, I'll take the photos of Whitey to all the Cable Beach Hotels and ask if anyone booked him in. If they did, I might get a name and an address."

Damien's and Jimmy's fathers thought the pearl farm tour a good idea, so the boys booked it at the travel counter then rushed off for a swim.

An hour later, wet-haired and hurriedly dressed they raced over the Japanese bridge to where the tour bus was waiting.

"Willie Creek Pearl farm is roughly an hour away," explained the driver as he drove through northern Broome and out into the uninhabited bush.

Damien and Jimmy stared at the flat grassland on either side of the road.

"So," said Damien, "tell me about these galloping stegosaurus."

"Glad to add to your education," said Jimmy in his best schoolteacher voice.

"There's nothing wrong with my education," argued Damien. "It's the best money can buy."

"Then how come you didn't know that a stegosaurus, from now on referred to as stego, was a plodder and not a galloper?"

"Got it," grinned Damien. "Continue, Professor. Please."

"Stegos roamed the world about 110 million years ago. They were non-aggressive vegetarian dinos with small reptilian heads, sloping shoulders, wide hips, short front legs, larger and heavier back legs and long tails. Four times the size of a hippopotamus, they were also the only armoured dinos to have different front feet to their back feet."

"Which is why the four matching footprints will sell for a load of money," emphasised Damien.

"Exactly. Stegos lived in herds sharing their swampy habitats with the much larger brontosaurus and the much small ornithopod. Ornithopods were two-legged plant eaters, podos meaning feat. Stegos' backs were covered in two rows of bony plates which they used for cooking and warming themselves, or for changing colour and attracting a mate. On their tail they had three or four spikes which they used for protection against the meat-eating megalosauropus. How am I going so far? Are you stunned by my superior knowledge?"

"Reeling with it. Were there cavemen around then?"

"No. Dinosaurs were long gone before early hominids appeared."

"Pity. It would have been fun to have been a caveman on a dinosaur hunt."

"You've been watching too much television, and it would not have been fun. Most dinosaurs could have outrun a caveman."

Damien flipped back his long hair and gazed out of the bus window. The landscape hadn't changed. "So how come the stegos left their footprints behind?"

Jimmy adjusted his sunnies then began again. This time in his best storytelling voice, "One hot day a stego family went for a walk along the sandy clay of the banks of their lagoon. As they plodded along, plod, plod, plod, they left behind big fat footprints, which hardened in the midday sun. The next day and the day after and the day after that, the wind blew sand into the footprints, filling them up and putting them to sleep. Millions of years later, after the land had subsided beneath the sea and risen again, cyclones revealed the stego footprints, which were supposed to stay there forever, only some of them were stolen."

"Cute," chuckled Damien. "So, if I was a fossil thief where else would I go to find fossils in Australia?"

"Queensland has dino tracks and fossils especially of Go Go fish. Victoria has fossil beaches and Dampier Peninsular is one of the world's richest sites for dino tracks. One day I'm going to dig in all of those places and who knows; I might discover a new dinosaur that will be named the Jimmyosaurus or the Jimmyopod."

"Dream on," teased Damien. But once again he was impressed with Jimmy's ambition. *One day I'm going to say something like that,* he decided. *And it is going to be just as important as finding a new dinosaur.*

With a large bounce the bus left the main highway and headed down an unsealed road. "Sometimes this whole area is flooded, and we have to go by boat," announced the driver, turning off onto a rutted dirt track that cut across a salt-marsh plain that looked as if it spent half the year under the sea.

Fifteen minutes later the driver pulled up outside the picturesque colonial-style Willie Creek Pearl farmhouse.

The house, made of northern Australia's favourite building material, corrugated iron, was painted white and its roof, lattice work and trellises were painted the same green as the coconut palms that surrounded it. It was a beautiful welcoming house, and the tourists couldn't wait to lounge in the raffia armchairs on the wide verandas, drink cups of tea and eat homemade damper. Across the lawn in front of the sparkling turquoise bay, was a sign that read, "Beware of Crocodiles".

Damien elbowed Jimmy. "Crocodiles!"

"Prehistoric reptiles," Jimmy corrected, elbowing him back.

"Quite right," said the driver, who'd been listening to them. "Crocs have been around for 200 million years. As a species they are older than the dinosaurs."

"See!" said Jimmy.

"Know it all!" said Damien.

The driver shot them a warning glance, then he spoke to the rest of the group. "First we will take a quick look at the pearl shop in case anyone wants to buy a soft drink or a million-dollar pearl. Then we'll take a trip on the *Willie Wanderer* where you will learn about modern day pearling techniques. Want to go to sea, boys?"

"Only if I can be a pirate," said Damien, smiling at the rest of the tourists and immediately winning the hearts of all the older women.

"Slimebucket," whispered Jimmy.

"Can't help it if I'm a charmer," grinned Damien.

As they had decided they would not ask about Sammy Jacob until they'd had a good look round, they did a quick circle of the shop, and then headed off to explore the nearby beach, when the driver called to them. "Don't go too far fellas. Some of the mud banks are none too safe or solid."

Damien and Jimmy nodded, then pretended to examine nearby, "We could ask the driver?" suggested Damien.

Jimmy eyed the driver through the palm fronds and nodded.

They walked back to the bus. "I was wondering if you knew a man called Sammy Jacobs?" asked Damien.

"Sure, everyone knows Sammy. He lives in a shack down the creek near the dumped Indonesian fishing boats. Sometimes he crews for *Willie Wanderer.* He's probably waiting for us now. Just follow the path to the jetty. I'll hurry along the others.

As they started walking along the jetty towards the white sailing boat, Damien stopped Jimmy. "What are we going to say to Sammy?"

Jimmy chewed on his bottom lip. "I reckon we show him the photo, tell him to go to the police and warn him about Abba's curse-man while we are on the boat and surrounded by people. He can't get violent with everyone watching, can he?"

"What if he threatens us the way he threatened Abba? Only quietly so no one hears?"

"Then we stick with the group and when we get back to Abba, we decide what to do next."

"Whatever we decide I'm in mega trouble. I can feel it," grumbled Damien.

"Not if we become local heroes."

"I'm not sure my dad is impressed with local heroes."

One by one the twelve tourists, with Damien and Jimmy in the middle, boarded the white yacht. Sammy was not one of the crew.

"Now what?" hissed Damien, as with a shout of, "Yo ho ho and a bottle of rum", the skipper turned the boat seawards and the *Willie Wanderer* set sail.

Ten minutes later they dropped anchor in Willie Creek Bay. Here, the skipper gave an informative talk on how in the olden days, pearl divers collected mother-of-pearl shell for shirt buttons and how any natural pearls they found were an added bonus. Then plastic shirt buttons were invented, and Broome looked like it would go broke until a Japanese man invented cultured pearls.

"Cultured pearls are made by seeding oyster shells with a small ball of plastic then the seeded shells are placed into thin wire panels and suspended in the creek day for forty days to let the shells head. An oyster can live for about four years and can be seeded four times."

The skipper held up a large metal frame with two slides of wire to keep the shells in place. "As low tides is about ten metres, these panels have to be strung together and hung where the water is deepest."

Jimmy found the talk interesting, but Damien, disappointed at not finding Sammy Jacob onboard, hardly listened until the boat was heading back to the jetty and the skipper pointed to four gutted boats lying in shallow water off a muddy beach. "Indonesian fishing or people smuggling boats. Confiscated for straying into Aussie territory," he told everyone.

"Let's go and look at the Indonesian boats," said Damien, the minute they were off the *Willie Wanderer.* "We've about an hour while everyone is having tea and damper and buying pearls."

Jimmy looked surprised, "Are you crazy? I thought the idea was to be surrounded by people when we confronted Sammy."

"It was," agreed Damien. "But the conference is over in two days, and we'll be gone; leaving Abba with Sammy still threatening her. Not only that, if my father finds out that I lied to him again, I would rather it be when you and Abba are around than when I'm in Melbourne on my own. So, let's find Sammy and warn him off, or are you too scared bro?"

"Of course, I'm scared, bro," exclaimed Jimmy. "Smart people are scared when there is something to be scared about."

"Spoken like a true hero."

Jimmy made a face at Damien's back as he followed him along a narrow track that wound through the mangroves in the direction of the beached boats. Very quickly the sandy track turned to a dry mud track with mangrove roots sticking up as if determined to trip them. Then dry turned to wet and the track became covered in insects, hovering over what looked like mud-crab claw prints, but which could have been a small crocodile's tracks. Then it turned into a squishy swamp where someone had placed planks of wood over the boggy, sour-smelling slush.

"This is not fun," complained Jimmy, brushing away in army of insects that had decided his fair skin and blond hair were worth attacking.

"Think of it as an adventure like on T.V.," said Damien, as his Reeboks sunk into the mud.

They were about fifteen minutes away from the Willie Creek farmhouse when they caught a glimpse of a stationary white ute.

"Keep your eyes peeled for Sammy," ordered Damien in his best detective voice.

"As if I wouldn't," muttered Jimmy. "I'm watching out for monster mosquitoes, giant snakes and man-eating crocs. Any of these planks could be one in disguise. Crocs look like planks when they're sleeping."

"Tick tock, tick tock," whispered Damien.

"What are you going on about?"

"Peter Pan's crocodile had a clock inside of him. Don't you know anything?"

"Shut up!"

Further around the mangrove-edged bay, the planks had been replaced by small rickety bridges and walkways. None of them looked safe.

"Probably First World War," said Damien.

"And probably half the time under a ten-metre tide," added Jimmy. Then he stopped. They both stopped and listened.

Damien couldn't hear anything other than the slurping of the mud under the decrepit walkway. "What is it?" he mouthed to Jimmy.

"Someone is behind us," Jimmy mouthed back.

"Wouldn't Sammy be in front?'

"Not if he saw us coming. Not if he has a mate."

"I hadn't thought of that."

Then Jimmy pointed at a building he'd glimpsed through the trees.

Damien narrowed his eyes against the glitter from the sea. On the edge of a muddy beach stood a dilapidated tin shed.

"Come on," he urged.

Jimmy followed him toe to heel. "What if he isn't there?" he whispered over Damien's shoulder.

"Then we will leave the photo, a message and my mobile phone number."

"We haven't got any paper to write a message on."

Damien patted the back pocket of his jeans. "What sort of palaeontologist are you going to make if you don't carry paper with you? What if we found a fossil and you had to draw it or write about it?"

"In this mud! It would probably be alive, and it would probably eat us."

It was then, as if his words had wished it to happen, that the planks under Damien slid sideways, broke in two and pitched Damien into the swamp.

For a second all Jimmy could see were ripples spreading out over chocolate-brown water. Then a dark head appeared, covered in slime and weeds, and Damien began to flounder about trying to swim in what looked and felt like thick chocolate sauce. The more he floundered the deeper he sunk.

"Help! Get me out of here! Get me out before a croc comes."

"Stop moving!" yelled Jimmy, racing back a few steps and breaking off a branch from a melaleuca tree.

"If I stop moving, I'll sink!"

Hanging onto the most solid part of the walkway, Jimmy stretched the branch out over the mud. Suddenly the planks beneath his feet began to creak and rock. They weren't solid at all.

"I can't reach it," gasped Damien.

Jimmy learnt out further. Then, as the tip of the branch brushed Damien's head and Damien lunged forwards to catch hold of it, Jimmy began to slide.

"Help!" yelled Jimmy as he joined Damien in the chocolate sauce mud.

Fortunately, Damien had caught hold of the branch that had become jammed between the sinking planks. He pulled himself onto the more solid part of the walkway, then held the branch out to Jimmy. Jimmy was stretching for it when Damien's head jerked up as he stared at something behind Jimmy.

*A croc,* thought Jimmy, *there's a croc in the water. It's going to attack me!* Then he felt two hands on his shoulders pushing him down. His mouth filled with muddy water as he went under to the sound of Damien yelling that he was calling the police.

The man was gone by the time Jimmy surfaced. Spluttering and spitting out mud he tried to touch bottom. There wasn't one, yet swimming in the thick sludge was almost impossible. Then he saw the branch waving in front of him and he grabbed it.

With Damien hanging onto the subsiding walkway and Jimmy hanging onto the branch while sliding up the submerged planks, Jimmy was heaved out of the mud.

"Watch...he...doesn't come back," he spluttered.

"I'm watching," yelled Damien as he grabbed Jimmy's T-shirt and heaved him further up the walkway, scraping the mud-covered boy's arms and legs.

Together they lay panting on the sagging planks like two prehistory amphibians enjoying their first trip on dry land.

"Yuk!" complained Damien. "I think I swallowed crocodile poo. I think I am going spew."

Jimmy grinned at him. "Me too. Was it Sammy who pushed me?"

Damien rolled over so he could see the walkway in both directions. "Couldn't tell. I only saw him for a second and I was more worried about crocodiles."

"Tick tock, tick tock," said Jimmy.

# Chapter 6

"What on earth has got into you?" shouted Padric West, turning off his laptop and slamming it shut. "That's the second outfit you've ruined in two days."

"It's not ruined, Dad, just wet. We had to get under the hose before we got back on the tour bus because we were covered in mud. It was an accident; the walkway fell apart underneath our feet."

"I don't want to hear any more excuses. I just want to know why, when I send my son off on an organised tour, he returns in ruined clothes. Perhaps it is the manager of the tour agency I should be talking to about firing his driver and replacing your clothes."

Damien looked down at his dirt-covered T-shirt and jeans. "It's only mud, I'll wash them."

"Don't you dare! I want to be able to show them to a solicitor."

"But it was my fault. I went on a walkway that I wasn't supposed to go on. It gave way and I fell into the mud. The driver wasn't anywhere near."

"A walkway you weren't supposed to be on. Great! Well, I've had enough of this rubbish. I'm ringing your mother and you're going to

London. It's her turn to take responsibility for you. I'd send you tomorrow only she's not there. She's on holiday. So, when do I get a holiday?"

"You don't take holidays," retorted Damien. "You work all the time."

"So how do you expect me to work if I have to worry about you every minute? Which reminds me, you can spend the last two weeks of your holiday at El Rancho camp. I'm not having you running wild around Melbourne."

"Not again. I'm too old for a horse camp."

"Plus, you're grounded until we leave here. Now for heaven's sake have a shower, you stink of mud. I'm going to dinner."

Damien showered, washed his clothes even though he knew it would cause another row, then lay in the dark thinking about London. Perhaps it wouldn't be so bad. After all, London had Buckingham Palace, Big Ben and the largest Ferris wheel in the world. But his mother had said that if his father insisted on sending him, he would not be living with her in London. So where would he be living?

He switched on the light and glanced at the room-service menu. He didn't feel like eating. His stomach felt strange. "I'm probably poisoned from swallowing all the mud," he told himself. "I'm probably suffering from croc-poo fever." Then he dialled Jimmy's room number.

"Hi. I'm grounded. What about you?"

"Mega grounded."

"Because of your clothes?"

"No. They've gone to the laundry. I'm grounded because we wandered into crocodile infested waters and suffered a near death experience. My dad hasn't stopped going on about it. Did you know that Western Australia has the largest number of freshwater crocodiles in the country?"

"Do freshwater crocs eat people?"

"No. But they get pretty big."

"I reckon it was saltwater croc country."

"Me too. Did you know that a predatory 'salty' moves faster than a racehorse? That they are nesting this month; that they are territorial and will defend their nests against all intruders, such as two stupid block-headed boys stamping around in the mud?"

Damien laughed. "No."

"Well, I do," continued Jimmy. "Because my dad googled it and has repeated it a thousand times. What about your dad? What did he say?"

"I'm to go to London to live with my mum after I have spent the rest of the holidays at a horse-riding camp."

"Oh!" Jimmy didn't know what to say in reply to Damien's flat unemotional answer. The he spoke up quickly. "One out of three's not bad. Horse-riding sounds good."

"I've been going there since I was five. If I see another horse I will puke."

"Better a horse than a croc."

"Says who?"

There was another silence, then Damien spoke again. "He didn't ask about crocodiles or drowning; all he went on about was my ruined clothes. I could have come home minus a leg and all he'd be worried about was my new jeans."

Jimmy definitely didn't know what to say to that. His father had demanded to know how much mud he'd swallowed, if his scratches were made by wood or old nails, if they hurt, and if his tetanus shots were up to date. He'd even rung Jimmy's mother to tell her, and Jimmy had answered the same questions all over again.

"So," continued Damien. "How do we let Abba know what happened? She should be warned that Sammy Jacobs tried to drown you."

"Us," corrected Jimmy. "Her mother is working on the reception desk tonight. I'll ring and ask her to get Abba to ring me. Pity your room is on the eighth floor--best view in the hotel and mine is on the first--otherwise we could shout to each other. My sisters do that when they are grounded."

"You never mentioned you had sisters."

"They are unmentionable."

Damien laughed and Jimmy made a thumbs up sign at himself in the mirror.

"Or I could just come down and visit you," said Damien. "I mean I have already got the ultimate punishment, what more can he do?"

Jimmy nodded at the telephone. "Think of it this way. London might be awesome. The National Museum has the best dinosaurs and you might be happier living with your mum."

There was a third silence that lasted so long Jimmy was about to ask if Damien was still there when Damien spoke in a voice even flatter and less emotional than before. "She's been gone for years. Her emails, which are about three lines long and three times a year, are always about her fashion business. Nothing about her. And her new husband hates teenagers. So although my father hates me, at least he doesn't have a girlfriend or wife who wants to poison my cereal. Would you get into more trouble with your dad if I came down now?"

"He's not here. But don't visit me yet. I have an idea. I'll get back to you. You'd better ring Abba's mother and tell Abba to contact you; a call from the eighth floor is more important than a call from the first floor."

As he dressed, Jimmy thought about how he might be grounded for another week and decided that his idea was worth it.

He found his father talking to some men in the tropical garden lounge. When he approached, his father's eyebrows rose questioningly, but he didn't reprimand his son for leaving their room. Instead, he introduced him saying, "This is Jimmy, my son," then aside to Jimmy, he asked. "Aren't you feeling well?"

Jimmy smiled at the men, then whispered back, "Can I speak to you in private. It's an emergency."

Paul Chadwick excused himself, and he and Jimmy walked out into the garden. Once alone, Jimmy told him how Damien was being punished by being sent to London to live with his uncaring mother and stepfather who hated teenagers.

"And it is unfair, Dad, because Damien only ruined his new clothes while saving me from drowning."

Jimmy knew that he was stretching the truth, but he could still remember how hard it had been to swim in the muddy water and he was sure that he would have drowned if Damien hadn't pulled him out.

"So, I thought you could talk to Mr. West and explain that Damien is a hero and that he shouldn't be punished."

Paul looked puzzled. "Run that bit about his new clothes being ruined past me again."

"First he wrecked his new clothes when he fell off the bike a couple of nights ago, then he wrecked a second lot today," explained Jimmy. "That's why he is being punished."

"Can't his clothes be washed?"

Jimmy shrugged, "I don't know. Maybe it's because they're labelled clothes, you know top fashion, or because his dad is fed up with him. Please dad, Damien doesn't deserve to be sent to London. Not when he saved my life. Can't you do something?"

"Okay. Okay."

Padric West was dining alone when Paul Chadwick and Jimmy approached him. "I'm sorry to interrupt your dinner, Padric," said Paul. "But I was hoping to see Damien. I wanted to thank him for saving

Jimmy's life. He was extraordinarily brave, and you must be very proud of him. It's a pity they don't give medals for that sort of bravery. It isn't every boy who would jump into a sinking mud bog to save another boy. Not into a quick-sand dangerous swamp full of pregnant crocodiles protecting their nests. No sir. That was an incredible brave thing to do."

Jimmy' father stopped talking and waited for Padric West to say something. But Damien's father was too astounded to say anything. So Paul continued. "As a reward, I was wondering if Damien could come and stay with us in Sydney for the rest of the school holidays. The boys get on so well and Jimmy could show Damien the Natural History Museum, he practically lives there. And I'd keep my eye on the both of them, I can assure you."

Padric West asked them to sit down. "This is all news to me," he said. "Please tell me exactly what happened."

While Padric West ordered coffee for Paul and a soft drink for Jimmy, Jimmy told him how he and Damien had wanted to find out more about the Indonesian fishing and illegal immigrant boats, as Jimmy had a project about it to finish before returning to school. So, they had gone along a walkway that had looked perfectly safe but wasn't. "Then it gave way and I fell into the swamp. The water was so muddy I couldn't swim. I was sinking and if Damien hadn't held out a branch to save me, I would have drowned. So, Mr West, can Damien come to Sydney? I'm doing some research on fossils, and he could help."

Padric West looked even more puzzled at this. "Do you really think Damien is interested in fossils?"

"Oh yes. He's very interested. It's all we talk about."

"Well then..." Padric West raised his eyebrows at Paul, "as our plane goes through Sydney on our way to Melbourne, I suppose a couple of weeks in Sydney wouldn't hurt. When are you leaving?"

"The day after tomorrow."

"Then I wonder if Damien could travel with you. I need to stay here a couple of extra days; and to tell the truth, we are getting on each other's nerves."

"Of course," said Paul Chadwick.

"Great!" cried Jimmy. "Can I tell Damien now?"

Padric West nodded. "He's in his room."

"We'll leave you to finish your dinner," said Paul, standing up and grabbing hold of Jimmy's shoulder before he could bolt. "We can make arrangements tomorrow."

They were back in the tropical garden lounge before he let go of Jimmy, "So are you happy now?"

Jimmy couldn't get his answer out fast enough. "I think you're great, Dad. I think you are the best father ever. I would never have thought of asking Damien to come and stay. It's a wicked idea, and I'm sorry I broke being grounded. I'll go back to our room the minute I've told Damien. I'll even stay grounded all tomorrow if you like."

"And do what?" laughed his father. "That school project on Indonesian fishing and illegal immigrant boats, perhaps?"

Jimmy looked guilty. "I thought it would help."

"It did. Only now it means Mr. West and I will expect to see a project say in...two weeks. So you can forget about being grounded. Go and tell Damien about Sydney. But remember his father didn't say anything about him not going to London."

Damien was lying in the bed feeling utterly miserable and wondering if a steak sandwich would help, when he heard a knock on his door. "Who is it?" he yelled.

"A bearer of very good news," Jimmy yelled back.

Damien was off his bed through the suite's lounge room and opening the door before Jimmy could shout again.

"I thought I was visiting you."

Jimmy grinned. "Yesterday's news. Want to hear today's?"

"Come in. Only you can't stay long because my dad would freak if he found anyone here. Although...I suppose it doesn't matter now. Still...he'd shout at you."

"No, he wouldn't. He said I could come up, and guess what? My dad asked if you could come to Sydney for the rest of the holidays and your dad said yes."

Damien was speechless.

"So," prompted Jimmy, "If you feel like kissing the ground I walk on, that's okay too."

"You are awesome!" gasped Damien, pretending to kiss the carpet. "I can't believe you did it."

"There's a price. You have to do a project on Indonesian fishing boats, and you have to stick to my story, which is that you are a hero because you saved my life. Talking about heroes, did you ring Abba?"

"I rang her mum and asked her to get Abba to ring me. I said I was sick from falling into a swamp and swallowing half of it. But so far, no Abba. I was just thinking about ordering a double steak sandwich. Do you feel like one?"

"I never say no to meat," said Jimmy. "Can I look around? Your room is three times the size of ours."

While Damien rang for room service and ordered two double steak sandwiches and to chocolate milkshakes, Jimmy explored.

"We only have a double room, bathroom and balcony," he yelled from the second bathroom. "You've got a whole house. Wow! Is this your own kitchen?"

"Yes. Only we never use it," said Damien. "We don't use our one at home either. We normally eat out, send for takeaway, or the housekeeper makes dinner and leaves it for us."

"You have a housekeeper!" exclaimed Jimmy, from the master bedroom. "I hope you like home-style baked beans on toast style cooking because that is what you'll get at our house."

"I love home style cooking."

Ten minutes later there was a second knock on the door and when Damien opened it. Abba was standing there holding a heaped-up tray. "I kidnapped your steak sandwiches and brought them us so I could see how sick you really are. You don't look sick. My mother said you sounded as if you were dying."

"I'm suffering from acute starvation and croc-poo fever," announced Damien.

"Hi Abba," shouted Jimmy from the depth of a huge armchair. "I'm suffering from mud poisoning and starvation. Want half a double steak sandwich?"

Abba placed the tray on the coffee table and lopped down in a second armchair that was so big it almost engulfed her. "Yes, I do. But what I really want to know is what happened at Willie Creek."

While Damien divided the sandwiches, Jimmy filed Abba in including the bit about Damien being sent to London.

"Only now that my dad thinks I'm a hero for saving Jimmy's life," interrupted Damien. "I might just be able to change his mind, if I don't get into any more trouble."

Abba glanced at Jimmy who made a hopeless face, then she asked, "So what are we going to do about Sammy? I mean, he hit and threatened me, and he nearly drowned you. We have to do something."

"Agreed," said Jimmy, handing her half his milk shake. "We're decided to write an anonymous letter describing everything. We'll post if from a post office in Sydney so the police can't trace the letter. Damien won't get into trouble and the police will arrest Sammy so he can't attack you again. What do you think?"

Abba hunched her shoulders, sucked at her milk shake straw, then she told them what she thought. "I only managed to get to three hotels with the photo of Whitey. No-one recognised him, so I reckon we should visit the rest tomorrow. Then, after you leave Broome and you have posted the letter, I will ask my grandfather if he told Sammy about the stegosaur footprints. If he did, I'll tell him how Sammy came to the house and scared me silly how he tried to drown Jimmy and how he's involved in the murder. If he didn't tell Sammy, I won't say anything."

Damien almost choked on his milk shake. "What if he tells the police?"

"He won't. Not if I tell him that an anonymous letter is coming. And not if he told Sammy about the location of the footprints because the curse-man will be after him as well as me."

Damien expression was dubious. "What makes you think your grandfather believes in the curse-man?"

"He was married to my grandmother for forty years. He knows Aboriginal law."

"What do you think he will do about Sammy?" asked Jimmy.

"He'll either go after him with his rifle, which I hope he won't because it is an old gun that can go off any time, or your anonymous letter will arrive and the whole town will know about Sammy because he will be arrested."

"Meanwhile, if we find out who Whitey is, we might be able to find out where the stegosaur footprints are," said Jimmy wiping his sauce-covered mouth with the back of his hand.

Abba handed him a serviette. "Which is something I really would like to do. Today I met some of my aunts and Uncles and they're predicting that the guardians of the songline will get sick if the footprints aren't returned, and it could be all my fault. They also said that Bob Cesar--that's the tracker--told the police and the local newspaper that one of the young people was wearing new jeans and a yellow T-shirt. He must have found threads or material from your clothes, Damien."

"Threads!"

"That's all Bob Cesar needs."

"Are they going to print that in the newspaper?"

"Don't know."

Damien sighed long and loud. "The faster I get out of Broome the better."

They talked about the footprints, the murder, what Damien and Jimmy would do in Sydney and how they wished Abba could be there with them, until ten o'clock. Then Abba said she had to meet up with her mum to go home, and Jimmy said he'd better be in bed when his dad came in.

"I'll walk you to your room," offered Abba.

They had reached the first floor before Jimmy got up the courage to ask Abba if she was sure there was no way she could come to Sydney. "My Mum and Dad wouldn't mind, and you could share with my sister Amber, she has twin beds."

"Nice thought," said Abba, linking arms with him. "But if I can't afford the tour to Willie Creek Pearl Farm, how do you think I can afford an air ticket to Sydney? Seriously Jimmy, my mum just makes ends meet."

His father wasn't in the room when he unlocked the door. Switching on the light he saw that his backpack and his father's case was open on their beds. Their clothes and his father's files were strewn all around the room as if a whirlwind had blown in through the open balcony doors.

"What the... I locked the balcony doors before I left."

"You've been robbed," cried Abba. "Don't go in. The robber might still be in the bathroom."

"I doubt it," said Jimmy, walking in as far as he needed to be able to look through the open bathroom door. There were towels on the floor and an open bathroom cabinet, but the room was empty.

"Ring reception," ordered Abba.

Jimmy rang and told Abba's mother what had happened. Five minutes later, Paul the hotel manager, the security manager, and a security guard arrived at the open door. Jimmy and Abba were on the balcony.

"We thought we'd better not touch anything," said Jimmy. "But it looks like he came in over the balcony. There is a knocked over plant pot, and the door lock is busted."

Jimmy told the manager and the security manager what time he'd left the room, what time he'd returned, and that he'd locked the glass doors to keep the room cool while he was away. It was established that the thief had climbed up to the first-floor balcony and jimmied open the glass doors. He'd stolen Jimmy's camera, Paul's laptop and his second mobile phone.

"And the photos," Jimmy whispered to Abba.

The manager was very apologetic. He kept insisting this sort of thing never happened at the Sunmoon Hotel. That they had an exemplary record of honesty and lack of robbery. That he was upset it should happen to Mr Chadwick and if Mr Chadwick would accompany him to his office to fill out the insurance forms, he would contact the police immediately so they could catch the thief and return their belongings to them. Meanwhile they would be upgraded to a suite on the eighth floor, and there would be no charge for their stay whatsoever.

While Mr. Chadwick went with the manager, Abba and Jimmy began cleaning up and packing.

"Ring Damien and tell him," said Abba.

"I bet it was Sammy," said Damien. "I'm coming down."

Jimmy replaced the phone. "He's on his way. He thinks it was Sammy, so do I, He also thinks my camera and dad's laptop will end up in Willie Creek Bay."

Abba agreed.

"Damn!" said Jimmy. "I liked that camera; it was an old Canon F-1 that I inherited from my uncle. It took stunning photographs."

"Were the negatives with the photographs?"

"Don't be crazy. The negatives are back in Sydney at the World Wildlife Fund's office. No photographer ever leaves his negatives with his photos just in case something happens, which it has."

Damien arrived a minute later. It was the first time Abba and Jimmy had seen him looking untidy and without his hair carefully combed to flop casually over one eye.

"Wow!" He exclaimed looking at Paul's files lying all over the floor. "Looks like Sammy did a good job of searching the place. Where were the photographs?"

"Under my pillow, I think he found them first and then threw the rest of dad's stuff around to make it look like a real robbery."

"Did he get the lot?"

"All accept the enlargement of himself which disintegrated in the swamp, and the photo of Whitey which Abba has."

"Which means Whitey won't know that we know what he looks like," added Abba.

"Good," said Damien. "Because if Whitey is as powerful as Sammy told Abba he was, then it will be very easy for him to find out where you live in Sydney because Sammy's bound to have seen your father's work address on his papers."

Jimmy' grey eyes grew large with shock. "Do you think they might break into my house? This is getting worse and worse."

# *Chapter 7*

They met next morning at the usual place. Abba was helping a man and woman choose their bicycles, telling them how far it was to Gantheaume Point and warning them that they would hit a dirt road half way there. Damien and Jimmy watched the couple ride off with the man wobbling all over the road.

"Don't reckon he'll make the dirt road," said Jimmy. "I reckon he'll wipe himself off around a palm tree long before that."

"One of those spiky, red-trunked ones," agreed Damien. "I can see the newspaper headline already. 'Tourist impaled on palm at Cable Beach resort. Wife impaled trying to free him'."

Abba giggled. "Stop it."

"So, what else do you have to do today?" asked Jimmy.

"Wait half an hour in case there are any more bike riders, then I'm free. Want to choose your bikes before the best ones go?"

The boys chose two bikes then waited while Abba helped four more people adjust the seats of their bikes.

At the end of the half hour, she closed the shed and fetched her bike from behind it. "There are four hotels left," she said. "Then we'll have to ride to town."

The receptionists of the four hotels listened sympathetically to Abba's story of how the man in the photo had run over one of her hotel bikes and how if she didn't find him to send him the repair bill, she'd have to pay for the repairs. But none of them recognised the white-haired man.

"What if he booked in late Wednesday night? Shouldn't we come back and ask the night receptionists?" asked Jimmy as they cycled away from the last hotel.

Abba turned towards Cable Beach. "The day receptionists would have seen him on Thursday morning when he booked out."

"Unless he went straight back to the hotel, packed up and left at one in the morning," yelled Damien, peddling after her.

"And go where?" she yelled back. "There aren't any planes until morning. And if he left that early the receptionist would have remembered, because it is suspicious."

She braked at the beach steps. "Do you feel like a swim before we go any further? I've got my cozzie on under my shorts."

Jimmy said he would swim in his shorts and Damien said he would cycle back and get his swimmers. While they waited for him, Jimmy and Abba sat on the top step and went over what they knew about the murder.

"Four men go to steal the footprints," Abba held up four fingers. "Sammy Jacobs, Whitey, Albert Thon who is now dead, and a fourth."

"Two are from Broome," continued Jimmy. "Both know about fossils and shells."

"The other two are fossil brokers from a city because they wore city shoes, which cuts out Darwin."

Jimmy's eyebrows rose questioningly.

"Darwin's a thong and sandal place," said Abba.

"Which leaves five cities, the three most likely being Perth, Melbourne and Sydney."

"Why those three?"

"Because they have fossil shops and because they're easy to fly out of with a suitcase, or in this case, a crate, of fossils."

Abba nodded to show this made sense. "Whitey and Thon argue over money. Whitey kills Thon. Sammy is left behind in Broome when Whitey and number four disappear with the footprints. Unless Sammy has hidden them somewhere until it is safer to move them."

"I reckon the broker would get them out of Broome. It's too small a town with too many curious eyes, and they did kill a local."

Abba agreed. "So, what we have to do is find out how Whitey and number four left Broome."

"I'm back," shouted Damien, braking his bike beside them. "Last in buys lunch."

"You're on," shouted Abba, throwing the bike lock to him. Kicking off her sandals she set off down the steps at full pelt, her brown legs flashing beneath her denim shorts. Next came Jimmy, his sunburnt and scratched legs pounding after her followed by Damien who after locking his bike, bounded down the stairs three at a time to catch up.

With Abba in the lead and the boys neck and neck, they raced across the wide expanse of sun-bright sand, cutting each other off tripping each other up and scattering sand all over the place, until panting and laughing they reached the water's edge. Here they stripped off their shorts, jeans and T-shirts, hid their moneybags under their clothes and galloped into the celadon-green water.

"I won," yelled Abba.

Damien splashed her. "No, you didn't. I did."

"You both cheated," yelled Jimmy, belly flopping beside them.

They splashed, dived, floated, and fooled around for an hour, then when they were all yelled out, they collected their clothes and money. By the time they'd crossed the sand and climbed the steps they were dry enough to get dressed.

The road into town was not wide enough for them to ride abreast so they rode single file, shouting to each other until they reached the first town motel. Two hours later, fed up with motel receptionists and guesthouse owners shaking their heads at the photographs, they decided to stop at the Courthouse Markets for lunch.

The Courthouse garden was packed. Beneath rainbow-coloured umbrellas there were about forty stalls selling paintings, artefacts, tie-dyed clothing, painted boomerangs, shells and photos of camels.

Clustered around the stalls were locals wearing baggy khaki shorts or tie-dyed ankle-length dresses and tourists. But it was the stall holders in their hippy outfits that astounded Damien.

"Look at their clothes, they're in a time warp," he exclaimed.

Abba punched him on the arm. "There's nothing wrong with their clothes. Stop being snobby. Not everyone wants to wear labelled clothes advertising the maker."

"She's not wrong," grinned Jimmy. "You're a walking billboard. Mambo T-shirt, Levi jeans, Calvin Klein socks, Reeboks, and I mean real ones not copies. They should pay you to walk around."

"Rack off," retorted Damien, but he wasn't angry. Somehow in Broome wearing the 'right' clothes didn't seem half as important as in Melbourne.

"So, what do you want?' asked Abba, as she locked their bikes together. "Sausage rolls, Thai food, steak sandwich or potato wedges."

"Chips and sauce," said Jimmy.

"Wedges and sour cream," said Damien.

"Thai and plenty of it," said Abba.

They separated and met under a mango tree where they sprawled on their stomachs and ate each other's food. Then they lay back on the grass in the shade and listened to the shrieks coming from the children racing around the stalls, and to the music being played by three different musicians in three different corners of the lawn.

"I was thinking," said Damien, raising his voice above that of an Aboriginal man singing Yothu Yindi songs. "Where would Sammy Jacobs sell his shells? Would it be here in the market?"

Abba shook her head. "No. These people have had their stalls for years. He most likely sells to souvenir shops such as Albert Thon's. Does anyone want any more Thai?"

"No thanks," mumbled Jimmy who was almost asleep.

"Yes please," said Damien.

Abba handed over what was left of her rice and chicken.

"Thanks." Damien filled his mouth, chewed, swallowed and continued talking. "That could be how they met to steal the footprints. But because they couldn't sell such big illegal items here in Broom, they needed a fossil broker, which is where Whitey and number four come in."

"Or it could have been that Whitey was given a wish list with stegosaur footprints on it. Whitey contacts Albert Thon, who contacts Sammy Jacobs, who knows where there are some footprints, either because he found them himself, or my grandfather told him," argued Abba.

"Who is number four?" asked Damien.

"Another fossil broker," muttered Jimmy. "Whitey would need someone to help him smuggle the footprints out of Broome and out of Australia, as they'd be too heavy for one person to move."

"Did Albert Thon have someone working for him or did he run his souvenir shop on his own?" asked Damien.

Abba lay back on the grass beside Jimmy. "He had a boy called Luke who cleans the shells, a salesgirl called Elise who is my cousin, and a Filipino wife who manages the shop. Albert Thon spent most of his time at the pub or at the betting shop or fishing for pearl shell, not always legally either."

"The how about we go to his shop?" said Damien. "If it's open we can show your cousin the photograph of Whitey."

Abba looked at Jimmy and rolled her eyes towards Damien. "He's not just a pretty face, is he?"

Jimmy grinned at the both of them. "Oh, I don't know about that."

"I'm not finished," smirked Damien. "After that we can ride over to the airport. If Whitey and number four left by plane on Thursday morning, then someone might remember them."

"What if they didn't leave by plane?" said Jimmy, wishing he had thought of the shop and the airport first.

"Then they would have had to drive out of town in a rented car because Sammy's ute is still here. So why don't we hit the car rental agencies as well?"

"What if they drove their own car or truck?" asked Abba.

Damien shook his head. "It wouldn't make any sense to drive all the way from Perth, Melbourne or Sydney; especially if you wanted to make a fast getaway."

"He's a genius," announced Abba, standing up and looking for a rubbish tin. Then, seeing Damien looking at her with a sceptical look, she added. "I mean it, Damien. You're good at this sort of thing. Have you thought of becoming a detective? You seem to have a knack for working things out."

Damien laughed. "You mean be a black-market fossil detective?" Then he looked at Jimmy. "What do you think?"

"I think your father would freak out. He's expecting you to be a high-powered, global-trotting businessman, not a stolen-bone tracker."

"True, but we don't all get what we expect in this life," answered Damien, glibly repeating words his father said to him on a daily basis.

But when the other two went in search of a rubbish bin Damien thought about what Abba had said, and he agreed with her. He really did like this detective business. But then Jimmy was right too, a bone-tracking detective was not a profession that would impress his father.

Albert Thon's shop was open for business under the management of Janie Thon, Albert Thon's widow. The only sign that Albert Thon was no longer living was a withered wreath hanging from the open front door beside the 'Open for Business' sign.

"Can I help you?" asked Janie Thon, hurrying forward the minute they stepped into the shop.

"Just looking," said Abba. "I'm sorry to hear about your loss, Mrs Thon."

"Not so much loss. Albert was running this shop into the ground. Now I'm in charge you will see big changes."

"Uh-huh!" nodded Abba, moving off towards Elsie who was dusting a bookshelf full of carved trochus shells and emu eggs.

"We're interested in fossil bones," she heard Jimmy say as he blocked Janie Thon from following her.

Abba sidled up to her cousin. "Hi cuz, can you do me a favour?"

Elsie glanced at Mrs Thon, saw that she was occupied with Jimmy and then smiled. "What is it Ab?"

Abba slid the photograph out of her backpack. "Did you ever see this man with Albert Thon?"

Elise's eyes flicked over the photograph then she quickly returned to dusting the shells. "Don't let her see that or there will be big trouble," she hissed. "I'll tell you later. Five o'clock at Aunty Rose's tree."

"I'm more interested in Gogo fish fossil from Fitzroy Crossing," Jimmy was saying when Abba joined them.

"Gogo fish?" Janie Thon repeated. "Aren't they those singing fish that people hang on the wall for a joke?"

"How could she not know what a Gogo fish is," he exclaimed the moment they were out of the shop. "Fitzroy Crossing which is only a bit north of here, has hundreds of square kilometres of Gogo fish fossils. Illegal Gogo fish fossils are top sellers at all the overseas fossil and mineral markets, especially in the USA."

"Elise knows something," interjected Abba. "We're to meet her after work. So how about we head for the airport? I need a dose of air-conditioning."

Broome airport was small and tucked away in a pocket of palms just north of the town. Abba said that it was normally deserted unless a plane was due in or about to leave, so they were fortunate to find a check-in clerk preparing for an early departure. She greeted Abba with a smile. "How's things, Abba?"

Damien nudged Jimmy. "Is this another of Abba's cousins?"

Jimmy laughed. "Probably. There are only about fifteen thousand people in and around Broome. She probably knows them all."

"I don't know fifteen thousand people in Melbourne."

"I don't know fifteen thousand people in Sydney. But rumour has it that country towns are friendlier. Let's edge up and listen."

The check-in clerk was examining the photograph. "Yes, I remember him."

"Do you know his name?" asked Abba.

"No, and no I can't look it up. It's private."

"Is it private to tell me where he flew to?"

The woman made a moue with her lips, then she noticed Damien and Jimmy listening.

"They're with me. It was the bike he hired that was run over," said Abba, pointing to Damien.

"I suppose his destination can't hurt. He and his friend went to Melbourne, via Alice Springs and then to Sydney. I remember them because they'd flown in only the day before and yet their luggage was really overweight. The man said he'd been buying up big to stock his Aboriginal souvenir shop, but later I asked Aunty and she said no one had been buying up big for months."

"Oh, and when I joked about how many boomerangs did one shop need? The second man snarled at me and barked, 'How many boomerangs is our business, not yours.' That put me right in my place, I can tell you. The strange thing is the police were here yesterday as well, asking for a list of the people who'd departed on Thursday and anyone with overweight luggage. Your questions haven't anything to do with that, have they?"

Abba tucked the photograph away quickly. "No. Did you tell them about the two men?"

"Sure did. Them and twenty others. Just about everyone leaves Broome with overweight luggage. They arrive with a couple of bikinis and a towel, and they take home half the Kimberleys. If I had a dollar for every didgeridoo, boomerang, carved totem pole or bark painting that they try to pass off as cabin luggage, I'd be rich. There was a woman last week who had six hand-painted cushions and a carved camel the size of a great Dane that she wanted to put in the overhead locker."

"So, what was the man who snarled at you like?" asked Abba.

"Foreign, they were both foreigners. He was shorter than the white-haired one who seemed to be the boss. He had no neck and muscles like a wrestler or weightlifter. Oh, and coarse hands. I noticed because when I handed him his seat ticked, they felt like sandpaper. I bet he's a bricklayer."

Abba nodded to all this then, while the boys wandered outside, she chatted for a bit longer about Albert Thon's murder, which was the main topic of conversation in Broome. Finally, she thanked the check-in clerk and slowly sauntered outside as if the information had been of no great importance.

The minute the glass doors shut behind her, she raced to her bike which Jimmy was holding for her.

"So they flew in on the day of the robbery and flew out to Melbourne the following morning," Jimmy said as he handed the bike over, "Which explains why we couldn't find them at a hotel."

"And the police have a list of all the people with overweight luggage," added Damien.

Abba nodded at both of them. "But don't you see? Whitey and number four would know the police would be checking up on overweight luggage so they wouldn't fly to where they'd bought a ticket to. They'd leave a false trail. They could have gotten off at Alice Springs or Sydney."

Jimmy shook his head. "Not Alice Springs, unless they were going to catch a plane to somewhere else. No-one would take stego footprints to Alice, but Sydney is a goer."

"Sydney is enormous!" moaned Abba. "And she wouldn't give us their names."

"Wouldn't matter if she had," said Damien. "They'd have been travelling under false ones."

Abba's cousin, Elise was waiting for them at Napier Park. Seeing them ride up, she broke away from a group of Aboriginal women sitting under a wide-branched baobab tree.

"Aunty Rose says hello," she told Abba. "Wave to her, or she'll be over here telling you off the way she's been telling me off ever since I got here."

"Hi Aunty Rose! How's it going?" shouted Abba, waving at the group, then aside to Elise. "Why is she cranky with you?"

"Doesn't like my boyfriend..."

Abba giggled. "She never likes anyone's boyfriends. She couldn't stand my father. She says if he ever comes back, she'll wack him on the head with a hula-hula for leaving us. Tell me, what do you know about the white-haired man?"

"Not much. But a couple of days ago..."

"Was it Wednesday?" interrupted Damien.

Elise nodded. "Wednesday afternoon, the man in your photograph met Mr Thon out the back of the shop where they couldn't be seen from the road."

"Was the white-haired man alone?" asked Damien.

"Yes. He looked as if he'd just flown in, because he was wearing a suit and his shirt was all sweaty."

"What were they talking about?" asked Abba.

"They were arguing over money. The man was saying that they had a contract and Mr Thon was saying he wanted double what was in the contract. The man said his client would not be pleased. But Mr Thon said that it was more money as soon as they got there or no deal. That plenty of others were interested. I guess they were talking about a bet. You know how Mr Thon was always betting on anything that moved. Anyway, their voices got louder and Mrs Thon heard them, and when Mr Thon came inside she gave him a tongue-lashing. Believe me, Abba, Aunty Rose has nothing on Mrs Thon when she is angry. She even threatened to divorce him if anything went wrong."

"So, Mrs Thon saw the white-haired man talking to her husband. Did the white-haired man see Mrs Thon?" asked Damien.

Elise shook her head. "No. She was peeping through the back window."

"What happened to the white-haired man?"

"He disappeared before she told her husband off and Mr Thon spent the next hour calming her down. I heard him say she wasn't to worry because soon they'd have plenty of money."

"Did you tell the police any of this?" asked Jimmy.

Elise shook her head. "Mrs Thon said if I told the police that she and her husband had argued on the day of his murder, or anything about the day of his murder, she'd fire me. She said nothing her husband did was the police's business. She and Aunty Rose agree on that."

"What about Sammy Jacobs? Did he have anything to do with Mr Thon or the man with the white hair?" asked Damien.

Elise looked surprised. "Sammy Jacobs! That thief! He hasn't been around since the dodgy pearl business."

"Did you hear Mr Thon call the man with the white hair by a name?" asked Abba.

Elise shook her head again. "No. But when Mr Thon came back into the shop, he was swearing about him. I heard him tell Mrs Thon that the man was nothing but a stinking Harbour Bridge rat, who thought he could come over here and push people around because he wore a suit."

"And you didn't tell the police that?" insisted Damien.

"No way. I need this job. Anyway, I'd rather have Mrs Thon as a boss than her husband. She upped our wages the minute she heard he was dead."

"Paid her to keep her mouth shut," said Damien as they wheeled their bikes away from the park.

"But did you hear what she said about Whitey? About him being a stinking Harbour Bridge rat?" demanded Jimmy, his grey eyes shining with excitement.

So. Whitey comes from Sydney. We'd decided that already," said Abba.

"Yes, but what you don't know is that there is a big shell and fossil shop right under the Harbour Bridge."

Damien and Abba stopped wheeling their bikes and stared at Jimmy, then Damien shook his head slowly. "It couldn't be that easy."

Jimmy's eager look disappeared. "I guess not. It does sound too easy, doesn't it?"

"Stop it you two," cried Abba. "Albert Thon sold carve trochus shells to the whole of Australia. If Whitey owned a Sydney shell shop, then that's how they met. It makes sense."

They were still going over everything when they rode into the Sunmoon Hotel and discovered a pile of bicycles dumped in front of the bike shed.

"What are you doing after you put them away?" asked Jimmy as he and Damien helped her untangle the bikes.

"I'm going home to wake up my mum, see if Grandfather Lou is back from fishing and have a shower. What are you two doing?'

Damien looked at Jimmy and then answered for both of them "We're going to have a swim, eat a huge dinner, pack our suitcases for our very early flight tomorrow morning then cycle over to your house to make the letter we are sending to the police. If that's okay with you?"

Abba smiled broadly at both of them. "Perfectly okay with me. Bring an old newspaper. We'll cut out the print. And take care riding bikes in the dark. Cars don't notice bikes at night."

"Unless they're white Toyota utes," said Jimmy.

"Then they aim at them," said Damien.

# *Chapter 8*

Abba rode up to the airport fence just as the Chadwicks and Damien were crossing the tarmac. In her bright red shorts and purple top, she stood out like a like house beacon amongst the tropical sun-bleached whites and beiges of the locals.

"Isn't that the girl from the hotel?" asked Paul.

"Yes." Jimmy waved at Abba. "She works there part-time. She's really nice, Dad."

"Is that so? Just remember what I said about girlfriends."

Jimmy felt his neck going red as he tried to ignore Damien's grin. "She's not my girlfriend, Dad. She's fossil freak like me."

"She's my girlfriend, Mr Chadwick," said Damien, his smile stretching even further as Jimmy' eyes narrowed.

"She is not!" snapped Jimmy.

"First it's crocs and now it's girls," said Paul Chadwick. "Seems like a good idea to leave Broome."

"I'll miss you both," yelled Abba, through cupped hands as they climbed up the mobile steps to the plane.

Jimmy glanced helplessly at Damien.

"We'll miss you too," shouted Damien. "We'll never forget you."

"Ummmmppph," grinned Paul Chadwick giving Jimmy a look that said *I'm glad it wasn't you who shouted that.*

"So how was the open-air cinema last night?" he asked as soon as they were seated.

"Full," Jimmy answered quickly, in case his father had somehow found out they hadn't gone to the cinema. That they'd gone to Abba's instead.

"What did you do all night?"

"Played computer games," said Damien. "I love computer games. Do you think I could get a glass of water, Mr Chadwick? If I don't drink something, I'll be airsick."

"I'll ask the flight attendant."

With the subject changed and Paul Chadwick preparing to work on his World Wild Fund notes, Jimmy and Damien plugged in their earphones and watched a science fiction movie.

They arrived in Sydney late in the afternoon after a long stopover in Alice Springs, and a second film which put Damien and Jimmy to sleep.

"They'll keep us both up tonight," Paul warned his wife as he loaded their luggage into the boot of the family station wagon. "Have you been waiting long?"

"Long enough," She gave his check a kiss and wriggled her fingers in a gesture of 'hello' to Jimmy and Damien. "You've grown Jimmy. Hello Damien."

"Hello Mrs Chadwick."

"This is Opal," said Jimmy, sliding into the back seat where one of his fifteen-year-old twin sisters was taking up most of the space. "Not that you will be able to tell them apart unless you've lived with them all your life."

"Then how do you know I'm not Pearl?" challenged Opal.

"Pearl is prettier. She's got prettier eyes and prettier lips, and she was born first and ..."

"Mum! He's being nasty."

"Stop teasing Jimmy. Damien, do you tease your sisters?"

"I don't have any, Mrs Chadwick. I'm an only child."

"That's sad."

"That's lucky," muttered Jimmy.

"But I wouldn't mind a sister who looked like Opal," Damien added, smiling at the pretty blonde girl squashed into the corner so that no part of her touched her younger brother.

"How sweet." said Mrs Chadwick.

"How slimebucket," muttered Jimmy, making a 'puking' sign at Damien.

"That's enough," said his father. "That goes for you too, Opal. You're old enough to know better."

Opal didn't say another word. She just sat there smiling sweetly at Damien while her fingers snaked over the car seat and pinched Jimmy's leg as hard as she could through his jeans.

The Chadwick family lived in a two-storied house which had once ruled over a large amount of land, that boasted of a prize-winning rose garden a fountain and stables for four horses out the back. But during the expansion of Sydney the land had been whittled away so that the house, looking a little worse for wear, now stood cheek to jowl with a row of terraces and a car showroom, while the stables had been bought and renovated into a town house.

Set back from the street, with the fountain, the only part of the large garden left, Jimmy' house reminded Damien of Abba's house. Then he realised why. They both looked like Bleak House in the film 'Psycho'.

"Any resident ghosts or monsters?" he whispered to Jimmy.

"Only the three Chadwick vampire sisters," Jimmy whispered back.

"Amber has cooked," Mrs Chadwick announced as she opened the front door and a cloud of spaghetti-sauce steam wafted over them. "So, I don't want any remarks, Jimmy. It's your turn tomorrow night. Damien can help. And no baked beans. I want a three-course dinner."

"I forgot to mention the cooking," whispered Jimmy as they climbed the stairs to his bedroom in the attic. "Mum has a business that keeps her busy, so we take turns to cook."

"What sort of business?" asked Damien, glancing with joy at the wonderful clutter that filled Jimmy' dormer window bedroom. His own bedroom was not allowed to be cluttered. His father hated a messy room. "A messy room means a messy mind," was one of his sayings. Their housekeeper agreed, so Damien never thought of his antiseptic-looking room as belonging to him. It really belonged to his father and the housekeeper.

"Mum runs a face-painting clown for parties' business. She has fairies too, and a tattooed-all-over man who knots balloons into animal shapes, and a man who dresses up as Dorothy Dinosaur's brother and sings Wiggles songs. I'll show you the costumes later."

"Do you get to be a clown?" asked Damien pointing to a photograph of Jimmy dressed as a clown.

"Only when she is desperate," said Jimmy as he removed shoe box after shoe box from his top bunk. "Opal and Pearl are better at face painting than I am. I'm good at somersaults and fooling around."

Damien watched him carefully stow the shoe boxes under his bunk.

"So, what's in the boxes?"

"Fossils. The top bunk is my museum. I don't get many friends staying over. They can't cope with my sisters."

"But Opal is gorgeous," gushed Damien, his blue eyes rolling ceiling wards to show how gorgeous. "She looks like an angel with all that curly blonde hair and those big grey eyes. I'd have thought you'd be the most popular boy in school for stay-overs."

"Wrong. Wrong. Wrong. As you will soon discover. It is no joke having twin sisters barely a year older than yourself and a prima donna sister three years older, who is having her final exam year mental breakdown." Jimmy threw a sheet at Damien. "Here, make your bed."

Damien met Amber and Opal's identical sister, Pearl, when they went to eat. Pearl was as pretty as Opal and Amber, even when hot and flushed from cooking, was utterly stunning. All three behaved beautifully to Damien while pretending that Jimmy was invisible.

"How come the four of you don't get on?" Damien asked when they were in bed that night.

"We did get on... until they became teenagers. And we do get on if anyone hurts any one of us. They're great protectors. I only have to mention to whoever is bothering me that I am related to the Chadwick sisters and all teasing about me being a fossil freak stops. And if they're in trouble 'cause they come in late, I help them, even to letting Amber climb through my window. It is just the day to day living that is difficult. The sharing of the bathroom for instance. And last year all the bottoms of my pyjamas disappeared because silk shorts were in fashion. I never saw them again. Then there are my fossils! If I'm not careful Amber will bore a hole through one of my best bones and wear it for jewellery. Girls don't get how important fossils are."

"Abba does."

"Abba is different. She's sort of...special."

"Will you two go to sleep!" shouted one of the twins from the room below.

"That's Opal," whispered Jimmy. "So, what are we doing tomorrow?"

"We are going to your dad's work to get your negatives, then to the post office to post the letter we made in Broome to the Broome Police. Then we're going to the Shell Shop to see if Whitey works there, or if the owner knows him."

"What if Sammy Jacobs told Whitey what we look like? We could be walking into a trap."

Damien though about this. "We'll case the joint first."

"We'll what?"

"Check out the shop."

"Will you two shut up!"

"That's Pearl," whispered Jimmy. "What do we do when we find Whitey?"

"We post a second anonymous letter to the Broome police telling them where he is and sending them the photograph of him."

Jimmy woke Damien at seven o'clock so they could be showered and breakfasted in time to get a lift to the World Wildlife Fund's office with Paul Chadwick. Damien was disappointed to find that the twins weren't up by the time they left.

At the World Wildlife Fund office Jimmy introduced Damien to the rest of his father's team, picked up the negatives and took them downstairs to the photo-developing shop to have two sets of photographs printed.

By ten-thirty they had posted the letter and were on the bus heading for the Rocks, a tourist area hull of special shops, convict-built hotels, terraced houses cobbled streets and outdoor restaurants nestled under the Harbour Bridge. The Shell Shop was open.

They wandered past it pretending not to look past the display in the window, but really staring into the interior.

"There's a salesman but it isn't Whitey." said Damien.

"Didn't expect it to be," said Jimmy. "Brokers don't own shops; not if they're into smuggling. They keep a low profile.'"

"What now?" asked Damien.

"You stay out of sight and watch to make sure Whitey doesn't come in while I am in there."

"And if he does?"

"Warn me."

Jimmy wandered into the shop. First, he fiddled with a tray of rose-quartz, then a tray of spider shells, while waiting for to tourists to buy a huge apricot-coloured conch shell. Then he examined a framed collection of butterflies until the shop was empty. The moment it was he approached the salesman.

"I was wondering if you sell photographs of dinosaur footprints?" he asked.

"Sometimes. If they're good ones," said the young man. "But not photos taken off the net. Anyone can do that."

"No-one can get these," said Jimmy, slipping four of the stegosaur footprint photos out of an envelope and onto the counter. "I got them just before they were stolen."

The young man looked interested. "Where were they stolen from?"

"Broome. About a week ago. The Aboriginal guardians are really angry. They've sent a curse-man after the thieves."

The young man laughed. "Got any more photos?"

Jimmy slipped six more out of the envelope, two of the photos were of Sammy Jacobs and Whitey.

The young man pounced on the two photographs. "Who are these men?"

"Oh! They aren't important," said Jimmy, plucking the photos from the assistant's fingers and putting them back in the envelope. "I took them at the same time. If you are interested in selling the stegosaur footprints on consignment, I can get more copies developed. There are four photos of the separate footprints, one of the front pair and one of the back pair and two of all of them. It's a good set."

The young man examined the eight photographs under a magnifying glass, placing the four single footprints on the counter as if a stegosaur was walking across it. Then he stacked the lot carefully and nodded. "I think I could sell them. Would six dollars a photograph be all right?"

Jimmy calculated fast and getting forty-eight dollars a set, smiled broadly. "Sounds good to me."

"So how will I get in touch with you if I sell these and want some more? What's your address?"

*Not likely*, thought Jimmy as he wrote down Damien' mobile phone number.

He was halfway out of the shop when the young man called out. "Have you got any more photos?"

His voice sounded odd and when Jimmy turned to answer, his face had a strange look on it.

"Not of stegosaurs. But there was other wildlife around alive and dead, that I photographed. But I'm not interested in selling those on consignment. I'd want a lot more for that set. So...." He began to back out of the shop. "Ring me if anyone is interested."

He found Damien sitting around the corner watching the Shell Shop in a car mirror. He looked relieved to see Jimmy. "What happened? Was Whitey there?"

"No. But when I 'accidently' showed the salesman his photograph, he behaved as if he recognised him."

"Could the salesman be number four?"

"No. Too skinny and too young; and he doesn't have an accent."

"So now what?"

"We wait until he calls your mobile. And in case he is ringing Whitey right now, we need a place to hide and watch in case Whitey heads over here real fast."

"Then what?"

"Then we follow Whitey."

They waited all afternoon. Nothing happened. By the time the Shell Shop closed, they were fed up with answering tourists' questions as to how they could get to Central Station or the Opera House.

"Do you want to see the Opera House before we head home?" asked Jimmy.

"Of course, I do. My dad is sure to quiz me about it."

So they walked home via the Opera House, the Botanical Gardens and the Kings Cross Supermarket arriving at the Vampire Den as Jimmy called it, in time to begin cooking.

"So, what's it to be, Maestro?" demanded Opal or Pearl from the kitchen door; Damien couldn't tell which.

"We're having leek soup, steak and salad and apple crumble," announced Jimmy. "Damien is chef, I am assistant."

"Can I help?"

"No. Rack off Opal. You'd just try to mess everything up."

"Mummm!"

"Leave the boys alone Opal," yelled her mother.

That night after a stupendous effort on both boys' parts, and a magnificent feast that astounded Jimmy' parents and his sisters and had them all insisting that Damien could live with them forever, the boys got onto the Internet. There was an email from Abba waiting for them.

*'Hi there you two. I've cleaned the bike shed and have no more work this morning. I miss you already, bicycle riding will never be the same. NEWS FLASH! Sammy Jacobs has left town. I asked my grandfather if he had told Sammy about the fossils. He said he hadn't because I'd said it was a secret. So Sammy must have found out another way. Then I told my grandfather THAT I had another secret that I couldn't tell him yet but that it involved Sammy trying to drown Jimmy into Willie Creek, and Sammy sneaking around our house giving me a scare (That's an understatement) and that I was afraid to go home alone in case Sammy came back. Grandfather was so angry he drove out to Willie Creek to tell Sammy to keep away from our house. But there was no Sammy and no ute and the people from Willie Creek Pearl Farm said he had left two days ago. Which I reckon was right after he attacked Jimmy. Have you seen Whitey? Have you found the fossils? Will I quiz Luke, the shell-cleaner at Mrs Thon's shop? Keep in touch. I feel so far away. Abba.*

Jimmy emailed back no to her first two questions and yes to her third, then he told her what they had done, which as Damien pointed out, didn't add up to much. Then Jimmy scanned all the photos into his computer and sent them to her, asking her to take them to an internet café and using

Hotmail and a false name and address contact all the dinosaur mailing lists that she could google and warn them that the stegosaur footprint fossils were stolen.

"That's in case the museum or police haven't done it already," he explained to Damien. "Now we just have to wait until Whitey calls."

"What if he doesn't?"

Jimmy frowned at his computer. "There are three other fossil and shell shops we can go to and there's the Internet. I could advise that I have the photographs, and word the advert so that Whitey knows I have a photo of him."

"It's getting complicated, isn't it?" said Damien.

"Yep. But the answer to that is we can just send the photos to the police and let them do the searching. But then, after they arrest Sammy, they would find out about us, and you'd be off to London before you could blink."

"Which is still on the cards; unless we find the footprints or the murderer or both."

Damien's mobile rang at midnight. Damien almost fell off the top bunk diving for it. From below he heard one of the twins swear and the other promise to scalp someone in the morning.

"Yes," he whispered.

"I'm very interested in your stegosaur footprint photographs." said a whispery voice.

Damien nodded hard at the dark shape that was Jimmy standing on his bunk so he could be face to face with Damien.

"I'm told that you have other photographs," said the voice.

Jimmy switched on the light above Damien's bunk so he could see Damien's face.

"Yes," said Damien.

"What would they be of?"

"Two men. One with short white hair."

"Do you know these men?"

"No."

"Why did you photograph them?"

"For money," said Damien, relaxing back a little as Jimmy climbed up beside him.

"Has anyone else seen these photographs?"

Damien thought about this and decided it was a test, so he answered truthfully. "One of the men in the photograph stole some of the photographs but not the negatives. Now he has disappeared."

"Anyone else?

"The shop assistant at the Shell Shop near the Harbour Bridge."

"Anyone else?"

"No."

"Anyone else know when and why you took the photographs?"

"No. Which is why they should be valuable to you," said Damien.

"How valuable?"

Damien was stumped. He and Jimmy hadn't discussed how much they would ask for the photographs. He glanced frantically at Jimmy who only hearing one side of the conversation hadn't a clue why Damien was looking so frantic.

Then Damien remembered how much Jimmy had thought the footprints were worth and he answered the whispery voice. "We want five thousand dollars. Not a lot when you think of how much the footprints are worth."

There was a short silence, then. "Negatives included?"

"Everything."

"That seems a reasonable sum. Where do you propose that the exchange takes place?"

"The Shell Shop."

"I don't think so," answered the whispery voice. "I'd prefer somewhere a little busier."

"On the Opera House steps."

"Too far from my car. Why not Centennial Park?"

"One moment," Damien covered the mobile phone. "He wants to make the exchange at a place called Centennial Park."

Jimmy shook his head. "Too lonely. Tell him the Sydney Town Hall steps. Tell him if Whitey isn't coming then the buyer has to wear something we can identify him by."

Damien repeated Jimmy's words, but the caller didn't like the idea of wearing anything too noticeable, he preferred to know who he was looking for. So, catching sight of Jimmy's clown photo, Damien told him to look for a short busking clown, and to carry a rolled newspaper under his arm.

"Agreed. What time?"

"What time?" Damien whispered to Jimmy.

"Two o'clock."

"Two o'clock," he repeated.

"I'll be there," said the voice. "You had better be there too. There are ways of tracing hotel guests and mobile phones." Then the phone went dead.

"He's right, there are ways of tracing mobile phones. My dad had it done when his company was threatened by a crazy environmentalist. So what are we going to do?"

"Well, I'm not dressing up as a clown," said Jimmy. "That would make me a sitting duck."

Damien put his mobile under his pillow in case the man rang again. "I feel like a sitting duck already. What if he is tracing my mobile this minute?"

"Then he'll get your Melbourne address. Didn't you say your father's apartment was in an electronically protected security block with cameras and grilles that can lock down the minute the security guards see anyone suspicious?"

Damien nodded. "But what if they've got your address? Your mum doesn't even lock the front door half the time."

"Will you two shut up before we come up there and strangle you?" shouted Opal and Pearl together.

"We could always set those two harpies onto them," giggled Jimmy.

Then in a more serious voice, he continued, "Sleep on it, Damien. Tomorrow morning we'll come up with an idea. And we'll lock the front door."

"I'm warning you!" yelled Pearl.

"She's the fierce one," whispered Jimmy.

# *Chapter 9*

Jimmy and Damien slept in the next morning and had a late breakfast. After Damien had apologised to the twins for his mobile waking them, the boys went on the Internet to tell Abba what had happened. Waiting for them was an email from her dated the night before.

*Hi there, super sleuths, received photographs and instructions. NEWS FLASH: I've just been to Albert Thon's shop to talk to Luke. He said Mr Thon and Sammy were good friends and that Sammy discovered something which excited Mr and Mrs Thon so much that Mr Thon was on his telephone ringing interstate all morning. Which makes you wonder about Mrs Thon. I have also posted (from the safety of Hotmail and a false name at the local Internet café) a search on the dinosaur mailing lists for anyone interested in buying four Australian stegosaur footprints, plus photographs of their site of origin. It's a wild shot but who knows Whitey might see it and respond I hope you like the idea. Abba.*

Jimmy replied, telling her everything including the midnight phone conversation, word for word, finishing with how they had no idea what to do next, but that he would not wear a clown costume no matter what.

"I have it," said Damien as Jimmy disconnected from the Internet. "We go to the Town Hall Steps and if it is Whitey we will recognise him. If it is someone else, we'll see the rolled newspaper. Neither of them knows what we look like, but in case Sammy has described us we can try to look different. Then, while one of us watches from the steps, the other sits in a taxi. Is there a taxi rank near to the Town Hall?"

Jimmy nodded.

"Cool!" continued Damien, getting more enthusiastic as he explained his plan. "When the man gets fed up with waiting and leaves, we follow him in the taxi. If he rings, which he is sure to do we tell him that the Town Hall wasn't a good idea after all, that it has to be the Shell Shop and it has to be tomorrow."

"What if he threatens us?

"What can he do? We're on the phone and we have the photographs. Meanwhile, we'll know where he lives or at least we'll have an address that he goes to, and when it gets dark, we can check it out. What do you think? Cool, eh?"

"Cool!" echoed Jimmy with far less enthusiasm. "Except, he might know where I live, and taxis cost a fortune."

"Sammy might not have told him where you live, and..." Damien patted his back pocket. "I've got two hundred dollars."

"What!"

Damien flicked back his long hair and smiled broadly. "My father was worried I wouldn't like it here so it's my fare home to Melbourne."

Jimmy swallowed his indignation at anyone not likening it 'here', and thought about how much two hundred dollars would buy. Then he thought of something else. "Did you hear what you just said?"

"About not liking it here? I love it here. I wish I could live in your house forever. I even love your sisters. I especially love your sisters."

"No. About your father being worried. You always say he never worries about you, and that he hates you. Well?"

Damien looked thoughtful. "Yeah. You're right. He was worried. Do you think he might be having second thoughts about sending me to London?"

Remembering that Padric West had not mentioned London when he agreed that Damien could go to Sydney, Jimmy changed the subject. "Let's find the murderer and the footprints first. And I'll have to sit in the taxi because the phone caller might be the Shell Shop salesman, and he will recognise me."

"Okay and I'll case the Town Hall steps. The second he walks away I'll race over to you, and we follow his car," agreed Damien.

"Will a taxi driver do that?" queried Jimmy, who was not used to taking taxis.

Damien pulled the two hundred dollars out of his jeans pocket and waved them under Jimmy' nose. "If you show him this he will."

Having made their plan, they went online to tell Abba.

Abba slipped a King Curly CD into her player then logged onto the Internet. She missed Damien and Jimmy already, and she wished she could be with them searching for Whitey. She began typing.

*Hi possums. ENORMOUS NEWS FLASH: I have just returned from an early morning visit to the Internet Café and guess what? I have received an answer to my 'Do you want to buy' message. It came from a John Sandstone, care of Hotmail. I am forwarding it to you. I reckon the sender thinks I'm Sammy or here's a long shot...Mrs Thon. I am going to find out which.*

Abba stopped typing and sent the message. She printed off a copy of John Sandstone's email before snatching up a spare T-shirt, she ran downstairs to the phone directory then, copying Jimmy, she stuffed the sleeves of her spare T-shirt into her cheeks and dialled the number.

The phone rang for a long time before it was answered by Mrs Thon.

"Thon's souvenirs. Can I help you?"

"I have a message for you," growled Abba, almost choking on the T-shirt as she read out John Sandstone's email. "Enough. No more money. Show me proof that you know what happened or shut up. Think of how you benefited. Remember three things. There are more hammers in the world and Broome is not that far away. And you are playing a very dangerous game." Abba paused, then finished with. "Do you understand this message, Mrs Thon?"

There was silence at the end of the phone then Mrs Thon shrieked at the top of her voice. "Don't you threaten me. Don't forget I know what you did to my husband." Then she shouted something in an Asian language and hung up.

Abba pulled the T-shirt out of her mouth and took a deep breath. Then she raced upstairs to her computer. She began a new message labelled. IMPORTANT. SCARY.

*Mrs Thon knows that Whitey murdered her husband.*

She described what she'd done and how Mrs Thon had reacted. Then she sent the email to Jimmy.

There were two emails from Abba, one labelled URGENT and the other IMPORTANT. SCARY. Jimmy read them out to Damien, who was lying on the bottom bunk. When he got to the last line he swivelled round in his chair. "Abba says Mrs Thon knows who murdered her husband. But when she yelled at Abba she didn't say anything about being given any money, so I reckon John Sandstone is Whitey and he thinks Abba's email was from Sammy. Sammy benefited by being paid for telling them where the footprints were. I bet Whitey thinks Sammy is asking for more money."

Damien disagreed, "I think Abba is right. I think he thinks it is Mrs Thon. She benefited by getting rid of a gambling husband and inheriting a shop. She also didn't tell the police about Whitey and Albert Thon's argument. I reckon Whitey thinks she's blackmailing him."

Jimmy ran his fingers through his blond hair, spiking it the way he liked it, while he re-read Abba's email. "Whitey mentions having paid someone money. But when would he have paid Mrs Thon? There wasn't any time between stealing the footprints at midnight and leaving Broome the next morning. And Mrs Thon wouldn't have known that her husband was murdered until the body was found, which was after Whitey and number four left, unless..."

"Unless she was out on Gantheaume Point at the same time as we were and she saw it happen," Damien finished for him.

Jimmy thought about this, then shook his head. "We would have seen her and she would have seen us, and when we went to her shop I'm sure she didn't recognise us. I still reckon Whitey thinks it's Sammy doing a double-cross."

Damien flopped back onto Jimmy's pillow. "Maybe he paid them both. What if Mrs Thon got in touch with Whitey after the police found her husband's body and demanded money to keep quiet about the argument Whitey and Mr Thon had earlier at the shop?"

Jimmy twisted back and forth on his computer chair. "Yes. But wouldn't the police have checked up on any phone calls made by Albert Thon before his murder or phone calls made by Mrs Thon after his murder? Wouldn't they have found Whitey's number?"

"What if Albert Thon and Mrs Thon had to ring Whitey's mobile? And what if Whitey has chucked it so he can't be traced."

Jimmy nodded fast. "Which is why Whitey thinks Mrs Thon is getting in touch with him over the Internet because she wasn't able to ring him."

Damien triumphantly punched the air, finishing with a "Yes."

Jimmy looked at him with admiration. "You know, Abba is right. You should be a detective."

"You're not so bad yourself," said Damien graciously. "And here's another brilliant idea." He sat up fast and bumped his head on the bottom of the top bunk. "Ouch!"

"Pride comes before a bump," said Jimmy.

Damien threw a pillow at him. "I bet Mrs Thon wants Albert Thon's share of the money before the sale of the footprints."

"My turn! My turn!" yelled Jimmy, throwing the pillow back at Damien. "And she couldn't tell the police about Albert and Whitey arguing because she knew they were selling the footprints to someone, which makes her an accessory."

"Wicked!" said Damien. "Although I did think you were going to say it was because she was afraid of Abba's curse-man weaving a grass curse around her shop."

Jimmy nodded. "Ah! The curse-man! Let us not forget the curse-man." Then his voice changed to a ghostly one and he began flopping around in his computer chair while holding his stomach and moaning. "Are Whitey or number four feeling sick? Are you feeling sick? Am I feeling sick? Aaaaah!" He groaned loudly as he fell to the floor in slow motion.

"What's going on?" shouted Amber.

"We've been cursed," Jimmy yelled back.

They set off for the city at one o'clock. It took fifteen minutes to walk across the park to the station and ten minutes by train to reach Town Hall station. Damien checked his watch as they climbed the stairs to the street. "We're thirty-five minutes early."

"It'll give us time to look around," said Jimmy.

"What if he is looking around as well?"

"We'll do it separately and try to blend in with the lunchtime crowd. And if it is Whitey, we know what he looks like."

The Town Hall steps were a favourite place for people to meet and office workers wanting to eat lunch in the sun, so the steps were already crowded when the boys arrived.

Damien was dressed as a tourist with his hair tied in a ponytail, a style his father had forbidden, and wearing one of Jimmy's caps back to front and a backpack with the Swiss flag on it. He wandered up the steps into the Town Hall. After a quick look at the famous ceiling painted for when Queen Elizabeth visited Sydney, he wandered out again. There was no Whitey in sight and no man with a rolled newspaper.

Jimmy, with his blond hair hidden under his hoodie and with his second-best camera around his neck, headed for the Town Hall's stone balustrade. Hoisting himself up onto it, he watched a busker playing a violin on the station steps below. The busker ore an oversized orange and green jester's hat which, Jimmy decided could be mistaken for a clown's hat. Pity he wasn't wearing the full costume.

At five minutes to two o'clock, Jimmy, with a quick glance at Damien, crossed the road and climbed into a parked taxi. In his pocket he had a hundred of Damien's dollars and ten dollars of his own, in case something went wrong...such as Damien not getting to the taxi in time before Jimmy had to take off after the rolled-newspaper man's car. Jimmy told the taxi driver that he was expecting his friend at any minute. The driver turned on the taxi's meter.

Two o'clock came and went, and there was no man with a rolled newspaper. Jimmy decided that whoever had been sent had left after not seeing a clown, and Damien was wondering how long he could loll about at the bottom of the steps talking to two girls when a man in an overcoat stepped off the pavement and walked up the steps. Under his arm was a rolled newspaper.

*Number four*, thought Damien, recognising the short, muscular figure of the man who'd helped carry the heavy-laden blanket containing a stegosaur footprint up from the rocks.

Damien watched the man disappear inside the Town Hall. "So what movie are you going to?" he asked the girls.

"We told you already, *Bleak Night*." Answered the one with freckles.

"Sounds good," said Damien as number four reappeared with a scowl on his face. Scrutinising the steps, he adjusted the newspaper then stamped down them to the pavement, brushing so closely to the freckled faced girl that she shouted. "Do you mind?"

Damien hid his face as number four leant over the balustrade and searched the steps below. But when number four swung round for a last look at the Town Hall, Damien was staring straight at him. Their eyes met for a second before Damien turned towards the girls saying. "If I wasn't busy, I'd come with you."

This remark caused the freckle-faced girl to giggle and the other one to say, "We haven't invited you."

Less than a minute had passed before Damien turned back, but number four was gone. Leaping up, Damien searched the steps, the busy street, the cars waiting at the red lights and the steps behind the balustrade. Number four was at the bottom of them arguing with the busker. The busker was shaking his head. Damien could hear the jingling of his hat's bells. Suddenly number four grabbed the busker's violin bow.

"Help!" shouted the busker.

Some people tried to help but number four pushed the busker backwards. The busker stumbled against his music stand and in his attempt to save it and his violin, his orange and green hat fell off and tumbled musically down the steps to the station.

Damien waved over at the taxi and gestured down the steps, then with a, "Sorry girls," he took off after number four, leaving the freckled-faced girl elbowing her friend sharply in the ribs. "Why were you so nasty? He could have come with us. He had lovely eyes."

Jimmy threw his ten dollars at the surprised taxi driver, and was out of the taxi and racing down a closer set of steps leading to the railway station before the taxi driver had time to yell, "What do ya think ya doin'?"

Damien was disappearing down the escalator as Jimmy pushed his ticket into the entry machine. Jimmy leapt onto the escalator and ran down them. Once on the platform he looked left and then right and saw Damien hiding behind a chocolate-vending machine. Jimmy raised his hands palms up, questioningly. Damien gestured with his head at number four standing further down the platform. With a thumbs-up gesture, Jimmy sat on a seat between two women and tried to blend in. A minute later the train arrived.

With a carriage between him and Damien and a carriage between Damien and number four, Jimmy stood close to the doors so he could see who got off the train at each stop. *There were only four stations before the end of the line, so which one was number four going to get off at?* He held up four fingers to Damien, who he could see through the adjoining glass doors. Damien was nodding when his mobile rang.

Glancing around to see who could hear him, he spoke into it. "Yes."

This time the voice was not whispering, it was yelling. "Where za hell are you?"

"To whom am I speaking?" asked Damien as the doors opened at the first station and he was almost bowled over by the people getting off and then getting on. Number four did not get off.

"Who do you zink you are playing wiz?"

"If this is who I think it is," said Damien as calmly as he could, considering his heart felt as if it was beating at a hundred kilometres a minute. "The Town Hall steps were too crowded. I couldn't tell if you were alone or not. You could have planned an ambush so that you didn't have to pay me the money, and it didn't help when you attacked the busker. I want a safer place. I want the Shell Shop."

"You little..."

Damien interrupted him. "Tell the white-haired man with the lethal hammer to ring me next time," then he pressed the off button.

Number four did not ring back. Nor did he get out at the next two stops. He got off at the end of the line, with Damien following hidden amongst a group of school children, and five metres back, Jimmy following Damien.

Hurrying out of the station, number four strode purposefully across the road to the underpass car park. Damien looked for a taxi rank. The only one outside the station was empty.

"What now?" hissed Jimmy, joining him on the footpath.

"He saw me on the Town Hall steps so you'll have to go after him. Get his car number in case I can't find a taxi."

Jimmy sprinted over the road to the car park. Number four was halfway across it, opening the door of a grey Mercedes. Jimmy took a photograph of it before stationing himself between two cars ready to take the car number as it passed.

Number four sat in his car talking on his mobile for about five minutes. His expression was wrathful, and his hand actions agitated, Jimmy was thinking how he wouldn't like to meet him in a dark alleyway when the Mercedes' engine started up and number four drove towards Jimmy's hiding place. At the same time, over the road, a taxi pulled up and Damien jumped into it.

"Wait a second," he told the taxi driver. "My friend is coming."

The Mercedes passed Jimmy, driving slowly enough for him to photograph the number, then it exited down a ramp onto the road. Jimmy sprinted across the park to the station.

"Here," yelled Damien waving though the taxi window.

Jimmy changed direction and raced for the taxi. Damien flung open the back door, and Jimmy scrambled in.

"It's the grey Mercedes, I've got the numberplate."

"Follow the grey Mercedes," ordered Damien.

"Is this a trick?" demanded the taxi driver.

"I'll pay you double if you don't lose him," shouted Damien, waving a hundred dollars at him.

The taxi driver grinned at the two boys. "This is on TV isn't it? There's a secret camera somewhere, isn't there?"

"Yes," lied Jimmy. "But you only win if you don't lose that car and if he doesn't see you."

The taxi took off so fast that Jimmy and Damien hit the back seat with a thump. "I can do it," boasted the driver. "I was a taxi driver in Hong Kong. Buckle up please."

The Mercedes turned east and sped along New South head Road. Behind it, staying two or three cars back, sped the taxi.

"He's going too fast," complained the taxi driver.

"He's angry," said Damien. Then to Jimmy, "He rang while I was on the train, I told him what we'd agreed. He was furious."

"He was ringing someone from his car, and he was pretty angry then too," grinned Jimmy.

"He's turning south," said the taxi driver, slowing down so it didn't look as if he was following the Mercedes.

Twice they lost the Mercedes only to find it when the boys had almost given up.

"Don't let him see you," warned Damien as number four turned his car towards Maroubra Beach.

Three streets late the Mercedes swerved into a narrow driveway and stopped.

"Go past him!" yelled Damien. "Don't stop!"

The taxi driver drove past.

"Number twelve, pink house pine tree beside driveway, next to house up for sale," said Jimmy.

"What street?" Damien asked the driver.

"Wolsey Street. Where is the TV camera? Where is the joke?"

Damien laughed. "Sorry mate. No cameras. Can you take us to Edgecliff please."

"No TV? No trick?" repeated the taxi driver looking disappointed.

At Edgecliff they paid the driver double his fare.

"No TV? No trick?" mimicked Damien as they walked down the steps of the park towards Jimmy's house.

"Do you think number four saw us?" asked Jimmy.

Damien shook his head. "There were other cars and taxis. And we lost him twice, so we weren't following him all the time."

Jimmy kicked a stick off a step. "You don't think it was too convenient, too easy? You don't think he saw our taxi when we got into those narrow streets?"

"Probably," agreed Damien. "But he wouldn't think he was being followed. Not after he caught the train."

Jimmy gave up, "So what do you do now?"

"There's no point telling the Broome police his address, because we don't have a photograph of him at the scene of the crime. So, we do what we planned, check out the house and see if we can find Whitey."

"When?

"Tonight. When number four goes out. We can peek through the windows and see if we can see anything suspicious."

Jimmy stopped halfway down the steps. "What if there is a security alarm or a guard dog? We wouldn't get a foot inside the front garden without half the world knowing we were there."

"Yeah. Yeah," agreed Damien, stepping around Jimmy and continuing down the steps. "But if he's an illegal fossil broker and he has the footprints hidden there, he wouldn't want warning bells and flashing lights going off and bring the police racing up to his front door, would he? He'd keep a low profile. Like his house. It looks ordinary enough. No-one would think he was an international fossil thief. So I don't think it would be fitted with noisy security alarms. And if it is. I don't think they would be turned on."

Jimmy followed more slowly, "But if he has the footprints hidden there, he wouldn't want the place unsecured in case they are stolen."

"No-one knows they're there, and they may not be. They maybe with Whitey. If he lives in Sydney. Or number twelve might be Whitey's house and the footprints are at number four's house. If he lives in Sydney. Or they could be out of the country. We won't know unless we have a look. Did you notice that the house next door has a big 'For Sale' notice? Maybe it is empty. Maybe it doesn't have any alarms. Which means it might be a good way of getting into number four's backyard."

They had reached the bottom of the park and were starting on the six-block walk to the Chadwick house before Jimmy spoke again. "What if number four doesn't go out tonight?"

"We can fix that. We can ring him and say we have changed our minds, that the Shell Shop is no good. Then we arrange to meet somewhere about an hour's drive away. He'll leave the house to go to meet us, and we'll have a couple of hours to check it out. What do you think?"

"I think you are mad but brilliant. No wonder you get into trouble at school," grinned Jimmy.

"I told you that in confidence," yelled Damien, his face flushing red.

"I haven't told anyone," retorted Jimmy. "It's just a personal opinion."

"Then keep your opinions to yourself."

"I will."

They'd walked a block in sullen silence when Jimmy rounded on Damien. "Why is it so important, Damien? Why can't we tell the police everything?"

Damien released his hair from the ponytail, shaking it so it flopped each side of his face, hiding part of it from Jimmy' earnest scrutiny. "It's important because if we give the info to the cops, they become the heroes. But if we find out where Whitey lives and where the footprints are, we're the heroes, and...my dad would be proud of me for once."

"Breaking into someone's house is one insane way to make someone proud of you."

"I said...look through the windows."

"Oh yeah. What can you see through windows? Who do you think you are fooling?"

They stood on the corner glaring at each other. Damien, taller, stood in his favourite cool position with his thumbs hooked into his jeans and Jimmy burrowed into his zip-up hoodie, as if burrowing deep enough he would disappear, or the problem would disappear. Then he spoke again. "Okay, I'll go along with it. With one proviso. If we can't get near the house because number four doesn't leave it, or if he does leave it and we can't find anything suspicious, we send photocopies of all the photos to the Broome police station, along with an anonymous letter about everything we know. Is it a deal?"

Damien was still angry at Jimmy's reference to his problems at school, so he stubbornly pretended to think it over.

Jimmy continued more urgently. "It has to be, Damien! If we don't find anything at the house there is nothing more we can do. And I'm not afraid, which is what you are thinking, I really do believe it is getting dangerous. Those men have your mobile number. A good hacker could hack into your telephone records and find your address. They could find out that Abba's Internet message came from a café in Broome and if they are in contact with Sammy, they'd know Abba's address and mine from the hotel robbery. The next thing you know they'll be breaking into my house looking for the photographs. What if my mum is there alone? Or my sisters?"

Damien grabbed one of Jimmy's waving arms. "All right! But let's give it a try first. If we fail, we'll do everything you said. In fact, we can give up on being heroes altogether and tell the police who we are and what we saw, if you like."

"What about you going to London?"

"If I'm a witness in a murder trial maybe my dad won't send me to London. Or if he does, maybe I'll have to come back."

"What about Abba's mother giving up her night job at the hotel, and the curse-man getting Abba and us for telling about the footprints?"

"You aren't serious? You don't really believe in a curse-man?"

Jimmy nodded to show he did.

"Then the curse-man should be pleased that we are making such an effort to find out who he is supposed to curse," said Damien.

# *Chapter 10*

It was Opal and Pearl's turn to cook. They had ambitiously decided to roast a leg of lamb. Only the roast was taking longer than planned, so the potatoes were burnt and the broccoli had turned khaki. With banshee shrieks the girls ordered the boys out of the kitchen.

"You sound like two vampires undergoing torture on a Spanish Inquisition rack," yelled Jimmy. Then he took off for the safety of his room with Damien close behind him.

"When did you hear the shrieks of two vampires undergoing torture on a Spanish Inquisition rack?" laughed Damien, as he fell panting on Jimmy's bunk.

"They're in one of my computer games," he said locking his bedroom door in case his sisters decided to attack. Then he turned on his computer and opened up his email. Abba had written again.

*I feel I am missing out on all the fun. How did the meeting with Whitey go?*

Abba stared out of her window. The edge of the cyclone had been buffeting Broome all day. On the other side of the veranda the rain was coming down in solid sheets of silver rain. It blocked out the palm trees, the bougainvillea, Broome.

"And the world," muttered Abba. Then she shook herself--she had never had this feeling of isolation before, so why now?

"Because I want to be in Sydney catching Whitey," she told her computer. She began typing again.

*NEWS FLASH: Police divers found a hammer wrapped in hessian off Gantheaume Point. It could have been bought anywhere but I asked Elise to check and see if any of Albert Thon's tools were missing. So far she hasn't gotten back to me. The newspaper says the thieves drove metal wedges in a straight line into the sandstone, and tunnelled under the rock layers with a broad-headed chise.l A few had whacks with the hammer and they had a perfect square of sandstone. They looked like professionals. The police think it was done by a stonemason. I discovered, while surfing the Net, that the global trade in stolen antiquities, meaning fossils, is the third largest criminal trade in the world after drugs and guns. Which is something you probably know, Jimmy. But did you know that there is an international agreed checklist for recording fossils in eighty-four different countries? Even New Scotland Yard uses it. Of course, our stegosaur footprints weren't catalogued. Thought I would mention the above, so you'd know what you are getting yourselves into. Be careful. Got another answer to my wanting to sell footprint's email. It said, 'Interested, contact Erebus'. What should I do?"*

Jimmy answered immediately giving her the Mercedes' numberplate and the address of the pink house. He also said not to answer Erebus, which was a reputable Fossil shop in central London and unlikely to be after stolen fossils, so the email might be a trick. Then, when Damien went to the toilet, he typed in a quick message labelled 'FOR YOUR EYES ONLY'.

By the time Damien returned he was into an archaeological theft site.

"Look at this," he pointed to an illustration and read the text. "The teeth of this 68-million-year-old Madagascan dinosaur were prised out of this unusual whirl of teeth by French fossil thieves, thus ruining a perfectly preserved jawbone'. Wow! I would have loved to have seen that jawbone. How could an animal eat with a whirl of teeth like that?"

"What's happening here?" asked Damien pointing to an illustration of an archaeological dig.

Jimmy read the text. "Due to constant pilfering from Chinese archaeological sites by farmers who sell the dinosaur bones as dragon bones to traditional medicine makers, government guards have been placed at the sites. Alas, those guards are all too willing to participate in the profits. Medicines that include the million-year-old ground-down dragon bones are sedatives and tranquillisers, taken for heart palpitations and insomnia."

"Yuk!" exclaimed Damien. "Fancy swallowing million-year-old dinosaur dust just to go to sleep."

"Here's a good one," continued Jimmy. "The whereabouts of certain bones belonging to Peking Man, which is thought to be the oldest hominid fossil in China, is still an unsolved mystery. Bet they're hanging on some rich collector's wall."

"Dinner," yelled one of the twins from the bottom of the stairs.

"That's Pearl," said Jimmy.

"How can you tell?" asked Damien as they headed downstairs.

"Dunno. Guess it's because I've had them screaming in my ear since I was born."

"Who's screaming in whose ear?" demanded Opal as they entered the kitchen.

One look at her red, perspiring face, untidy hair and the carving knife she was holding, and Jimmy decided that silence was the better part of valour. A quote he'd learned from his Mum since she'd been dealing with Amber's final-exam hysterics.

"Rock singers hurt my ears," he lied. "Hi Mum. Hi Dad."

"Hello Mr. and Mrs. Chadwick, hello Amber. That looks good, er, Opal? Pearl?" said Damien gesturing to the kitchen table where a frizzled-up leg of lamb sat on a large serving dish, surrounded by a ring of small black potatoes next to a plate of unrecognisable broccoli.

"Are you making fun?" demanded Opal. Or was it Pearl? Damien couldn't tell.

"No. I love homemade food. All I get at home is takeaway Thai food."

"Perhaps we could have takeaway Thai food tomorrow night," said Paul Chadwick, sawing away at the leg of lamb.

"Good idea," said his wife, whose turn it was to cook. "You can choose what we have to eat, Damien."

After they'd finished eating and Damien and Jimmy had stacked the dishwasher, Jimmy asked his father if he and Damien could go out. "Where to?"

"The cinema, a walk around the city, bus to the beach," answered Jimmy vaguely.

"Well make up your mind. And I don't see why not," answered his father, already heading for the newspaper. "Home by ten-thirty though."

"Can we come?" asked Pearl, whose good nature was completely restored now their dinner was over.

"No," said Jimmy, glancing to see that his father was out of earshot, "How can we meet girls if we have sisters hanging around."

"Oooooh! Jamie's going to meet girls," teased Opal.

"Damien! I though you liked us," teased Pearl, gently pinching Damien's cheek. The gesture was so unexpected that Damien blushed.

"Ignore them," ordered Jimmy, dragging him away.

"We can go out tomorrow night," called Damien as Jimmy closed the front door.

"Not with me they can't," retorted Jimmy.

"Why not? And why'd you say we were meeting girls?"

"It's the only way I can get out of the house without those two. Honestly Damien, my sisters are dying for me to meet girls so they can gossip about it."

They walked a block then hailed a taxi to take them to Maroubra.

"Shouldn't we have dressed in black?" said Jimmy as they left the taxi at the end of Wolsey Street.

"Too suspicious looking," Damien answered seriously.

"I was joking." But he wasn't. He was worried.

Wolsey Street was quiet and peaceful. The streetlights threw golden circles around the cars parked along the kerbs. Oblong house lights shone out between curtains lighting up neat gardens, and there was the sound of televisions. But there were no lights on inside the house that was up for sale or in number twelve, and the Mercedes was no longer in the driveway. Instead, there was a large white van squashed in between the wooden side fence and a pine tree.

"He's out," said Jimmy with relief.

"Unless he is in one of the back rooms," warned Damien. "We'll have to go carefully until we are sure."

"So, what's with the van, do you think?"

"Maybe he's moving. Which makes sense if you thought two different people were blackmailing you and one had incriminating photographs and the other was the wife of the man you murdered."

"Right, so is it up the pink house's driveway or up the 'For Sale' house's driveway and over the fence?" asked Jimmy, trying to sound braver than he felt. Because suddenly he didn't feel brave at all. It wasn't because what they were doing was against the law, especially as number four was a crook of the first degree and they were trying to catch him; it was because common-sense told him that international criminals did not let teenagers fool with them. Nor did international criminals leave their houses unguarded. This house didn't even have security grills on the windows. Something wasn't right.

Damien scanned the street, then checked his watch. "It's almost nine, so there is no time to fool around. We'll try number four's driveway. If we're seen, we can say we are visiting friends and got the wrong address. No-one visits an empty house up for sale."

Picking their way over the pine needles they walked up the driveway trying to look as if they were visiting, while being as quiet as possible. They were squeezing past the van when Jimmy noticed the original printing on the passenger side had been spray-painted over and the word 'Furniture' had been painted on top in blue.

He touched the paint. It was still wet. "Number four hasn't been gone long. This paint is sticky. Why do you think he painted over the van's name?"

"Because he doesn't like the name it had. Because he doesn't want the van's advertising to be noticed. Because..." Damien stopped and squinted at the side of the van. He could just make out the words under the white paint. "Because I think we have just found our stone cutter. The van used to have a sign that said, 'Crazy Paving and Stone Cutting'. Is that a good enough reason for you?"

"Sssshhh. We're visiting, remember."

The front door was at the side of the house. Beside it was a fence with a gate. The gate was not locked.

"It should be locked," warned Jimmy.

Damien slowly pushed the gate open. "Maybe he left in a hurry. Maybe that's why the van's paint is still wet."

They crept through the gateway and around the side of the house. The backyard was overgrown. It didn't look like the backyard of a wealthy international criminal.

"Damien!"

"Sssshhh. I'm going to check the door and windows."

The back door was locked. So were the back windows. But on the far side they found an open bathroom window.

Damien shone his torch inside There was a towel on the floor and some clothes hanging over the shower door. It looked as if someone had showered in a hurry.

"I'm going in," he whispered. "Bunk me up."

Two minutes later, he opened the back door for Jimmy.

"The place is full of packing boxes. He's definitely on the move." Jimmy switched on his torch and tiptoed after Damien. The first room was a sunroom furnished with cane chairs and a coffee table. On the coffee table was a box of multi-coloured spray-cans and a large plastic bottle of superglue.

"What's with the superglue?" whispered Damien.

"Fossil finders coat the newly exposed bones with it to stop them from cracking and flaking," whispered Jimmy.

"What about these?" Damien focused his torch beam onto the sunroom's walls. They were covered with state maps of Australia; the fossil areas were circled in red.

"They're the locations of fossils. They are locals, Australians," whispered Jimmy. "They know where everything is."

The next room was the kitchen. It was spotlessly clean and appeared to have not been cooked in for some time. The third room, the largest, was a mess. Half-packed boxes were open all over the floor, and the only furniture was a fold-out table with a computer on it, a dining table and a row of specimen drawers.

Jimmy shone his torch beam onto the dining table. It was covered with clusters of round grey stones resting in packing-paper nests, and flat round stone laid out on cotton wool.

"Dinosaur eggs and Lovenia," he whispered.

"Love...what?"

"Fossilised sea urchins."

"What about this?" Damien shone his torch at the specimen drawers.

Resting against the drawers was a large slab of stone with the fossil of a dinosaur embedded in it.

"Shine your torch closer," cried Jimmy, shining his own torch onto the slab.

The skeleton was twisted as if the dinosaur had died in pain. Around its bones were fine wispy depressions that could have been feathers. Where its stomach should have been there was a small rolled up skeleton.

"Is it a bird or dinosaur?" whispered Damien.

When he answered, Jimmy's voice was brimming with awe. "It's a pregnant Confucius ornis, or a pregnant pterosaur."

"What's it worth?"

"If it's not a fake, a winged reptile is worth about forty thousand USA dollars."

"Why would anyone fake a dinosaur fossil?"

"For forty thousand USA dollars, dimwit! Or for fame. In 1912 a skull was found in a quarry near an English town called Piltdown. Everyone thought it was the missing link. It fooled a lot of palaeontologists. But in 1954 it was discovered that the human cranium had been stained to look ancient and the jaw and teeth were from an orang-utan."

Damien grinned. "I bet someone looked silly."

"They sure did."

Jimmy looked around the room. "You know, this looks like a fossil warehouse. I bet these boxes are for posting off dino eggs and fossils. In fact, the stegosaur footprints could be here, about to be put into that van and taken off somewhere to be shipped overseas."

"You're right. I'll be back in a minute." Damien headed towards the back door.

"Where are you going?"

"Tell you later."

Jimmy continued exploring the room and was staring down at a pale-yellow object larger than a football nestled in shredded paper, when Damien returned. He pointed at the yellow object. "What is it?"

"It's a Madagascan elephant bird's egg. I thought there was only one specimen in Australia."

"Then you were wrong," said a voice. Jimmy spun round. Before he could see who had spoken a blanket was thrown over his head an arm tightened around his neck, and he was kicked in the back of the knees. As his legs buckled, he felt something hit his head and his skull exploded. His last thought was...hammer.

Swinging his torch as a weapon, Damien leapt upon the dark figure wrestling with Jimmy. He didn't hear the footsteps of the second man until a blanket was thrown over his head.

The man wrapped his arms around Damien, bear hugging him so tightly that he squeezed all the air out of Damien's lungs. Damien gasped for breath and fought back as he was swung off his feet. Still kicking backwards, his heels connected with the man's shins. In retaliation the man squeezed so hard that Damien's head spun and he blacked out.

When he came to, his arms were bound to his sides, with his hands tied behind his back, his ankles bound together, and his eyes and mouth taped over. *It must have taken forever to wrap me up like this,* he thought. *Must have used a whole roll of masking tape. How long had he blacked out? Was it half an hour? An hour?* He shook his head to clear his mind. Concentrate. Where was Jimmy? Was he wrapped up like a parcel too? Was he alive? He hadn't looked alive when he'd sagged against his attacker.

"Jimmy," he called through the tape. All that came out was a muffle squeak. He listened, hoping to hear an answering muffled squeak. There was none. But there was noise going on outside the room. Furniture and boxes were being slid across the floor. Number four and his friend were moving out.

*Got to get out of here. Got to help Jimmy. Think. Find a wall. Roll.* Damien rolled in one direction and hit a bed. He rolled in the other and hit a wardrobe. That would do. Placing his head against the wardrobe, he bent his knees and began edging himself upwards into a sitting position. Once sitting, he pushed his back against the wardrobe and levered himself up until he was standing.

From outside there came a loud bang as if someone had dropped something. Someone swore. Damien's stomach lurched, then churned. It was the same feeling he'd felt when they'd been in the pool with Sammy standing above them and the body floating towards them, signposting where they were to any passing crocodile.

*Wish my father was here,* he thought. *He would know what to do. He would be able to fix things.* His father was a great fixer. He never panicked. He just did what he had to do to succeed. *If he was here that's what he would tell me to do. Stop whingeing, Damien. Just do it and succeed.*

Walking was impossible, but if he wriggled his toes and then his heels he could inch along. He'd reached the middle of the wardrobe when he felt the wardrobe key. It stuck into his side just above the sick feeling in his stomach. The key was higher than his hands, and as he couldn't move them upwards, he wriggled back a bit so he could bend over.

*Big mistake,* was all he had time to think as he pitched forward into the dark, twisting just in time so he landed on his hip and shoulder and not flat on his face. "Ouch!" He groaned, as the pain in his hip spread down his leg. It was like doing a bellyflop into a pool without water. He lay on the carpet catching his breath and then he started again.

It seemed to take forever but he guessed that it took about fifteen minutes before he was standing against the wardrobe feeling for the key with his elbow. There it was. Good. This time he wouldn't over-balance. Slowly, he bent at the waist. The masking tape keeping his arms rigid was wound so tightly that it hurt. Finally, he felt the cold metal of the key against his cheek. Turning his head towards it, he began to rub the tape stuck across his mouth against the key. Each time he rubbed the key caught the edge of the tape, lifting it a little.

His back ached, his ears twanged and his heart thumped every time a sharp noise came from the lounge room. If the men came back and caught him, he'd probably get hit on the head the same as Jimmy.

He judged it took about half an hour before the tape tore enough for him to move his lips. "Jimmy," he whispered. There was no answer. Another ten minutes and he could squint through a tear in the tape covering his eyes.

He began to wriggle around the room, his fingertips feeling the smooth wardrobe doors, the wall, the bedroom door. It was then he realised that he couldn't feel his mobile. It had been in his hip pocket. Now it was gone. Had it fallen out when he was struggling? Did the men have it?

"Jimmy," he whispered again.

This time he heard a muffled sound.

"Keep talking," he whispered as he wriggled away from the wall.

More sounds, and Damien felt something soft on the floor in front of him. *Here goes,* he thought as he fell forward onto Jimmy.

Jimmy groaned. Damien rolled off him.

"Sorry. Can't kneel. My legs are stuck together. Had to fall. Where are your hands?

Jimmy rolled onto his side and his bound hands hit Damien's chin.

Damien began to bite through the tape. It took a long time. The tape was wrapped around at least five times, and Damien's jaw was aching from rubbing his face against the key, but at last Jimmy's hands were free.

Damien rolled over to so that his bound wrists were close to Jimmy's hands. "Undo mine," he whispered.

Half an hour later they had torn off all the tape and Damien was asking Jimmy about his head.

Jimmy felt it gingerly. "There's lots of sticky blood and I have a thumping, drum roll headache. But I'm not floating face down in a pool. So, let's get out of here."

Quickly and quietly, they checked the room. But although there hadn't been any security grille on the outside of the windows, there were bars on the inside. And the door handle, which Damien turned slowly, was locked from the outside.

Damien pressed his ear to it.

"Can you hear what they are saying?" Jimmy breathed into his ear.

Damien shook his head and gestured to the far wall where they could speak and not be heard.

"They took my watch and my mobile," he whispered as he crouched down beside the bed. "Do you know what time it is?"

Jimmy shook his head. "They took my watch too. But at a guess, we entered the house at nine. We looked around for about twenty minutes, which means they grabbed us before nine-thirty. After that I don't know how long I was unconscious."

Damien nodded. "They must have been expecting us. They must have known we followed number four. Whitey was probably following us in the train and then in the taxi. It was a set-up, a trick." Then he waited for Jimmy to say, "I told you so." or "it's your fault" or "If you weren't so hung up on being a hero we wouldn't be in this mess."

But Jimmy didn't say anything like that. All he said was, "I think you're right." Then he continued working out the time. "How long did it take you to get free?"

"About an hour. So, at the latest it's about ten-thirty."

"Then we have an hour."

"What for?"

"When I emailed Abba the last time, I told her to ring your mobile number at eleven-thirty our time, not Broome time. If you didn't answer, she'd know we were in trouble, and she was to ring my dad and tell him everything and give him this address. As proof I left the photographs sitting on my computer keyboard. So, all we have to do is wait for an hour.

"Why didn't you tell me this before?" demanded Damien.

"Because we might have been home by eleven-thirty. And because if you thought my dad might ring your dad you would have freaked out."

"Will your dad ring my dad?"

"Don't know."

From outside the door came a shout. "I'll check to see if they're awake."

"Quick, lie on the floor as if you are still tied up," hissed Damien, throwing himself flat on the floor. Jimmy did the same.

The bedroom door swung open. The light from the lounge room outlined the white hair of the tall man standing in the doorway and shone softly on the dark shapes of the boys lying still on the floor.

"Got yourselves together, have you?" said the man. "Well don't make yourselves comfortable. There's been a change of plan. At first, we were just going to leave you here tied up and useless, then when the rent ran out in a couple of weeks, the real estate people could find you dead or alive. But we've decided you might have told someone about this house, so we're taking you with us. Don't worry, we will dump you somewhere safe - safe for us that means, somewhere where you can't tell anyone anything."

Then he slammed the door, and they heard him shout, "They're okay. How much longer are you going to be?"

"Ten minutes. We'll be out of here by eleven ben-thirty," shouted number four.

# *Chapter 11*

Abba couldn't believe it. She was sitting on the bottom stair with her eyes glued to the clock waiting for it to be eleven-thirty in Sydney before she rang, when her grandfather walked towards the phone.

"No," was all she had time to shout before he'd picked it up and was ringing some tourist who wanted to hire his boat for a deepwater fishing trip the next day.

He talked on and on. First about what sort of fish they would catch. What sort of safety raft he had and what sort of bait they should use.

"Grandfather Lou, please hurry," she whispered. "I've got a really import..."

"This is important too, Abba. This is income."

So, she waited, tapping her fingers on her bare knees and softly drumming her bare heels on the polished boards.

Then, just as her grandfather put the phone down and Abba's fingers were reaching towards it, her mother rushed into the house, the front door slamming behind her. Snatching up the phone she dialled the Sunmoon

Hotel's number. "I'm in big, big trouble, Abba," she explained. "Big trouble."

The hotel receptionist answered, and Abba's mother spoke urgently into the phone. "Sofie, I left the safe keys in the woman's washroom on the ground floor. Yes. Yes. I'll hang on. Please, please find them."

"Oh no," groaned Abba as the big hand on the clock moved past the time she'd calculated was exactly right. "Mum, please hurry."

Her mother didn't seem to hear, then she let out a huge sigh and smiled at her daughter and father. "Wonderful. Yes. See you tomorrow."

Then to Abba. "What are you doing up so late?"

"Ringing Sydney," yelled Abba, lunging for the phone before her mother had time to put it down.

The minute they heard the key turn in the door locking them in again, Damien was on his feet looking around the dark room. "We need something to fight them with. I'll check the wardrobe. You check the drawers."

There was nothing in the wardrobe or the chest of drawers. Not even clothes.

Damien was under the bed looking for something, anything, when the door opened again. This time the bedroom light was switched on.

"What the... They've gotten free!"

"Shut the door," ordered number four.

The door slammed shut and the boys heard the key turn again. A couple of minutes later it was flung open, and number four and Whitey entered with more masking tape.

Damien slid further under the bed as the men ran at Jimmy. Jimmy yelled and struggled, and Damien heard Whitey threaten to hurt him so badly that he wouldn't wake up for a month if he didn't shut up.

Quickly, Damien slipped off his Reeboks and pulled off his Calvin Klein socks. Stuffing them into the wire mattress above his head, he made sure one toe was hanging out, then he slid his Reeboks on again.

"Your turn," yelled Whitey, grabbing Damien ankle and dragging him out from under the bed.

That was when a mobile phone began to ring.

"Merde!" yelled number four. "Where is it?"

"In your coat pocket," yelled Whitey, as Damien kicked number four in the shins and got a slap around the head for it.

"Watch him," shouted number four, thrusting Damien at Whitey. Then he unlocked the door and raced across the lounge room to where his overcoat was lying across the table. Searching through the pockets he retrieved the mobile and switched it on.

Abba listened impatiently as the phone rang. It rang five times before it was picked up. No one spoke. All she could hear was heavy breathing at the end of the line.

"Maybe he doesn't want to wake anyone," she whispered to her watching mother and grandfather. Then she glanced at the clock. It was exactly eleven-thirty in Sydney.

"Damien? Damien, is that you?"

Number four grinned back at Damien who was now being held in a neck lock by Whitey. He waved the mobile at him to let him know it was his, then he switched it off, but not before recording Abba's phone number. Then he rang another number.

Damien heard him say "Zis is Sydney. I have the bogus footprint seller's number." Then he said Abba's number followed by, "I don't care if you are no longer in Broome. Get back there and check out this number and silence whoever it is. Ozerwise Darwin won't be far enough away for you. Understand?"

Abba stared down at the phone, then she hung up and raced up the stairs.

"You do know the cost of a phone call to a Sydney mobile, don't you?" called her mother.

"I'll pay."

Grabbing up her address books she flicked to Jimmy's Sydney number and raced down the stairs again.

She didn't care who picked up the phone, Jimmy's father, mother or one of his three sisters, she just wished they would hurry up.

"Jimmy, is that you?" demanded an angry male voice. "Where are you, it is after eleven-thirty."

"It's not Jimmy, Mr Chadwick, it is Abba from Broome. And I'm afraid Jimmy and Damien are in incredible danger."

Then she told him everything.

Damien's one thought was to waste time to give Abba time to ring Jimmy's father and the police. If he could waste enough, the police would arrive before, he, Jimmy and the van had left the pink house. So, he struggled and wriggled and slid out of a surprised Whitey's neck grip. Over the double bed he leapt, over the bound-up Jimmy on the mattress trussed up like a chicken.

"Get 'im!" shouted number four, locking the bedroom door and racing around the bed so that Damien had a man coming from both sides.

Damien yelled as loud as he could and when they grabbed him, he struggled, kicked and punched, but number four had muscles of steel-- especially in his fingers, which he had pressed against Damien's windpipe.

"Bring ze ozer one," ordered number four as he hoisted Damien onto his shoulder. "We leave now."

With his eyes bound and finding it hard to breathe, Jimmy was tossed into the van on top of Damien who had been thrown in on top of three large suitcases lying on their sides. He heard the passenger door open and number four curse the narrow driveway as he crawled across the passenger seat to the driver's seat. Then he heard Whitey say something and the passenger door slammed shut. Jimmy tried to sit up but when the van started up with a jolt, he rolled off the suitcase onto the metal floor.

*I'll do what Damien did,* he thought. *I'll find something sharp to cut the tape from around my eyes and mouth.* But the van was swerving too much and he, Damien, and the three suitcases--the only items not tied down and protected by felt rugs and blankets--kept sliding from side to side.

At last, the swerving stopped and the van stopped. *Red light,* thought Jimmy, but then he heard the passenger door open and Whitey shouting about following the van in the Mercedes. The door slammed again, and the van jolted off again. This time they were going along a straight road which allowed Jimmy to jam himself between the two suitcases and wriggle into a sitting position.

*Try to imagine where the van is going,* he told himself. He listened as best he could through the tape. First, he picked out traffic sounds, then he counted how many times the van stopped for traffic lights. After a while the traffic became louder and the stops more frequent and he guessed they were in the city.

Ten minutes later the swerving began again, only this time the van was going much faster. Too fast, thought Jimmy, as a suitcase slammed into his side and a box above his head teetered and fell, hitting his shoulder. *At this rate,* he decided, *we are going to collide with something - a car, a lamp post, the corner of a building, and all the fossils will be wrecked.*

Then he heard sirens. They sounded a long way off, but the van accelerated. Soon the sirens sounded as if they were getting closer. Finally, they sounded right next to the van, but the van didn't slow down instead it swerved, did a rocking two-wheel-off-the-road circle and smashed sideways into something. The impact made more boxes fall on top of Jimmy and Damien.

Jimmy was lying with a box on his stomach and one on his legs wondering what had happened to Damien when the back of the truck was opened, and a voice shouted. "Remove the boxes fast lads, here is one of them."

Jimmy felt hands on his feet and the boxes being removed. "Is Damien all right?" he gasped as the tape was cut from around his head.

"They're unwinding him now," said the policeman.

"They beat him up."

"He's all right. You look pretty beaten up yourself."

Jimmy nodded in agreement. Every part of him hurt, especially when he waved his numb arms about to get the feeling back into them. "How did you find us?"

"Your friend in Broome sent the number of the Mercedes to a Mr Chadwick, who rang us with an unlikely kidnapping story. Especially when the police officers arrived at the Wolsey Street house and found it empty. But a thorough search revealed a pair of Calvin Klein socks with one of your names and addresses sewn onto them. Meanwhile the Broome police confirmed that stegosaur footprints were stolen. So all Sydney police were alerted to look out for the Mercedes. But it was the message written on the side of the van that did it. The bridge toll attendant saw it and rang us and we blocked off the other end of the Harbour Bridge."

"What message on the side of the van?" demanded Jimmy.

"See for yourself," said the officer, leading him to the crumpled side of the van where the words 'STOLEN GOODS, RING THE POLICE' were spray-painted in red paint.

Fifteen minutes later Jimmy and Damien were delivered to the hospital to be checked all over. It was here that the entire Chadwick family descended upon them like a brood of clucky hens.

"I can't believe it, Jimmy," exclaimed his mother hugging him tightly. "I can't believe you did all those dangerous things."

"I can't believe it either," added his father, in a serious wait-until-I-get-you-home voice. "Those men were murderous thugs, Jimmy. What were you thinking!"

"Just as well your girlfriend from Broome rang," said Amber, standing between the boys' beds so she could clasp a hand of each of them.

"Hi there hero," Opal hugged Jimmy like a protective mother bear.

"Hi there, you too hero," cried Pearl hugging Damien, carefully so she didn't hurt his bruises.

"Did they find the stegosaur footprints, Dad?" asked Jimmy.

"I imagine you will find that out tomorrow when you are interviewed by the police. They caught both men and are holding them for suspected murder and kidnapping."

"Suspected murder," laughed Damien tiredly. "Try definite murder with a hammer."

The next morning Jimmy and Damien were woken by a nurse wanting to take their temperatures and get their autographs.

"Autographs," mouthed Damien to Jimmy.

"Autographs," chorused Pearl and Opal, coming through the door. "You are famous."

"Mum and Dad are picking up Damien's dad from the airport," Opal informed them. "Amber is so annoyed at having to go to school. Especially with so many handsome reporters outside our house wanting to interview everyone. There's a man from a TV Channel who wants you on his show. He said we could be on it too..."

"We were allowed to stay so there would be someone here when you woke up," interrupted Pearl, thrusting a pile of newspapers at Damien. "See, you're on the front page."

Damien stared blankly at the newspapers. "Did you say my father was coming to Sydney?"

Opal nodded. "So is Abba and her mother. The TV station paid their fare."

"Did your father tell my father everything?"

This time it was Pearl who nodded. "Dad rang him last night and repeated what Abba had told him. He also emailed him copies of the photographs Jimmy left on his computer keyboard. Yuk! The one of the body is gross. Bet you took it Jimmy."

"I did," said Jimmy proudly.

"Did your father say what my father said?" persisted Damien.

"Only that he is catching the first available plane," said Opal. "Why? Do you think you'll be in big trouble"?"

"I don't think; I know I'm in mega trouble. I was safer in the murderer's van."

"You can't be in trouble," said Jimmy. "If you hadn't hidden your socks and written on the van, we could be anywhere now. You're a hero, Damien."

"Jimmy is right. Look at the heading of the newspaper," Opal held up the front page. It said, 'Boy's sock gives vital clue.'

All the other newspapers had similar headings and stories gleaned from the police officers and the excited twins. But although the papers made much of the teenagers' efforts to find the stolen stegosaur footprints, it was Abba, Damien and Jimmy's dogged pursuit of the murderer and his accomplices through crocodile-infested waters that had caught their interest.

"Dad told them about the crocodile-infested bit," grinned Pearl.

Padric West was not quite so enraptured with his son's exploits as were the twins or the newspaper reporters.

"You could have been killed," were his first words as he entered the hospital room.

"No, he couldn't," butted in Jimmy before Damien could answer. "Damien is really smart at getting out of things, Mr. West. And he is really good at working things out."

"Maybe so, but attempting to blackmail a murderer isn't very smart," snapped Padric West.

"We weren't blackmailing him Dad," explained Damien. "We were trying to find out where he lived so we could find the stolen footprints."

"Oh yes, the stolen footprints that started this whole thing."

"Have you heard anything about them?" asked Jimmy. "Were they found in the van?"

"No, they weren't," said his father from the doorway. "But thanks to you three capturing the fossil dealers, the police have traced the footprints to Europe."

"Which is not good," continued Jimmy' mother. "Because once a fossil is smuggled out of its country of origin it can be legally sold. Which I don't think is right, but that is how it is. What do you think, Mr. West?"

Padric West stared in bewilderment at Jimmy' mother and father, then he answered in a rush. "What do I care about a few fossils, when my son could have been murdered?"

Damien took a big breath and spoke up quickly. "So does this mean I still have to go to London, Dad?"

Jimmy, Damien, Opal, Pearl and Jimmy's parent watched the different emotions cross Padric West's face, then he answered. "We'll have to talk about that at the hotel."

"Hotel!" cried Damien. "I thought I was staying with Jimmy."

"That's another thing we have to talk about."

# Chapter 12

"That's her," shouted Damien as Abba came out of the airport's arrival doors followed by a pretty brown-skinned woman. "And that's her mum. You must have seen her at the hotel, Dad. She's the night receptionist."

"No," answered Padric West, smiling across the airport at the pretty woman. "I would have remembered her if I had seen her."

"Abba," shouted Jimmy, racing towards the slim teenager wearing a new pair of jeans and a 'Welcome to Broome' T-shirt. Damien raced after him. Behind them cameras flashed, and the crowd of reporters surged forward.

"Back please," ordered the policeman. "This is a police witness. No questions, please."

The three met in the centre of the marble floor. For a second Abba looked embarrassed and Jimmy looked nervous, then Damien, flicking back his hair, flung his arms around Abba and hugged her. She hugged him back until he yelped with pain, then she hugged Jimmy.

"I'm so glad to see you two alive," she said, linking arms with each of them. More cameras flashed.

"I couldn't believe it when I rang, and that awful man answered."

"He rang someone in Darwin and told them to get you," said Jimmy.

"That was Sammy. The police picked him up on his way to Broome. And they picked up Mrs Thon for knowing about the murder and obstructing police."

"You'll be obstructing the entire airport if we don't leave now," said Jimmy's father as he ushered Abba and her mother through the crowd of reporters to the Chadwick's station wagon.

"See you back at our house," yelled Jimmy, as Damien's father led Damien away to a company car.

Once assembled at the Chadwick's house, the five adults sat in the lounge room discussing the robbery, kidnapping of their children, the children's forthcoming television interview, and the fact that the Natural History Museum wanted them to speak at a gala dinner to raise funds for their palaeontology department.

Upstairs, squashed into Jimmy's bedroom, sat the six teenagers, with the twins and Damien on Jimmy's bottom bunk, Amber on the top bunk and Jimmy and Abba on cushions on the floor.

"So can you come back here for the rest of the week?" demanded Jimmy.

Damien nodded. "As long as I don't do anything stupid. And let me tell you, my dad's list of what is stupid is very, very long."

"What did your dad say about London?" asked Pearl.

"At first he wouldn't say anything. It was spooky. I could hear the hotel walls breathing. Then he said he couldn't imagine my mother putting up with all the television fuss, so I had better stay with him."

"Yeah!" shouted the twins.

"What about when you told him that you had decided to study to be a detective when you leave school?" asked Jimmy.

"I told him, then I waited for him to explode and be sarcastic the way he usually is, but all he said was that being a detective was a good profession and never dull, but if I was serious about it, I had better be more serious with my studies. Then..." Damien made a funny face. "He hugged me. I can't remember him every hugging me before."

"Wow!" sighed Abba. "How did you feel about that?"

"Weird...but nice."

Jimmy slapped hands with him. "It helps to be a hero."

"It certainly does," chorused Opal and Pearl, both hugging Damien so that all three almost fell off the bunk.

"So how did you write the message on the side of the van?" asked Abba grinning broadly at a squashed and red-faced Damien. "Jimmy said it was parked right up against the adjoining fence."

Damien wriggled out of the twins' embrace and slid down onto the floor beside Jimmy. "I climbed up on the house-for-sale side and spray-painted it on from there. That's why number four didn't see it. He had to get in from the other side."

"And what happened to the horrible man that frightened you, Abba?" asked Pearl.

"Sammy was caught driving from Darwin to Broome. He's in jail like the other two. They're all being accused of murder."

"And the footprints?"

"I know this one," cried Amber, swinging her long legs over the side of the top bunk. "I heard the police telling Dad. They said thanks to our heroes they know who the international dealers are, and they know which museum has the footprints. But the museum isn't admitting to anything so it doesn't look as if the footprints will be returned."

"So Abba," joked Damien. "Does your curse-man have a passport?"

Abba's dark eyes gazed into his blue ones and she gave a slow smile. "Curse-men don't need passports," she said softly. "They just go."

## You can find ALL our books up on our website at:

*http://www.writers-exchange.com*

## All our Young Adult Novels:

*https://www.writers-exchange.com/category/genres/young-adult/*

## All Patricia's Books:

*http://www.writers-exchange.com/Patricia-Bernard/*

# *About the Author*

**I** grew up in Melbourne and Rosebud, Victoria and had a great life full of adventure and freedom. I had a dog called Pal and a bicycle called Tonto. With Pal in my bike basket, I rode everywhere. Our family had Manx cats (that's cats with no tails from the Isle of Man) and a horse.

When I was eighteen, I travelled with my best friend Janet up the east coast of Australia picking fruit, getting lost in the Blue Mountains, learning how to be a waitress and working in Worth's Circus.

When I was nineteen, I went with my mother to England on THE BIG TRIP. I worked in London as a kindergarten teacher and a youth leader then I travelled all over Europe picking tomatoes in Spain, grapes in France, cooking on a boat from Barcelona to Mallorca, dating a bullfighter in Granada, eating Dutch pancakes in an attic whilst working in a Dutch lolly factory, taught English in Athens, ate 1 penny soup in Morocco, became a footpath artist in Paris and a nanny in Sweden for the Royal Family of Stucklebergs. During this time, I met three lifelong friends, Jeannie a crazy English girl and Dina and Robyn two insane Australian Spanish dancers. I then went to Canada and the U.S.A. on my way to Brazil.

In Canada I met my Jamaican husband on a staircase, which is why I always thought he was taller. I didn't reach Brazil until ten years later. We had 4 children, one in Jamaica, one in London, one in Geelong and one in Sydney, 3 girls and 1 boy.

On returning to Australia and realising I had been insane to stay away from the sun and the lifestyle for so long, we settled in Paddington, Sydney.

Years later I sent my middle daughter to Jamaica for one year's boarding school. She came back so much nicer having seen poverty and how hard Jamaican's study to get ahead. She is now a well-known public speaker/motivation and conference organiser for Landmark Education travelling throughout Australia, New Zealand, U.S.A. and India. My eldest daughter is also a motivational speaker and Course Leader for Landmark Education and has spoken to over 400,000 students throughout the world. My third daughter is a schoolteacher in the Blue Mountains and my son is a personal trainer. I have five brilliant grandchildren who I put in my books--see 'Legend of the Three Moons'.

I always sketched, painted, kept diaries and wrote letters when travelling, although my spelling was so bad no one could understand them. When I was thirty, a friend, Fiona, asked me to write a book for her television show. After I explained how badly I spelt, how I didn't know where to put a comma or how to start a paragraph, I started writing

RIDDLE OF THE TRUMPALAR. Thirty-eight books later I am still writing.

Her Writers Exchange website is: http://www.writers-exchange.com/Patricia-Bernard/

## If you want to read more about books by this author, they are listed on the following pages...

# Dinosaur Murder

{Young Adult Thriller}

Broome, north-west Australia--where rust-red cliffs meet a turquoise sea and 120-million-year-old dinosaur tracks emerge at the lowest tides.

Seventeen-year-old pearl-fisher's granddaughter Abba Lou guards a secret: four perfect stegosaur footprints hidden beneath weed-slick water. When she finally shares them with visiting fossil-freak Jimmy Chadwick and businessman's son Damien East, the tide delivers a drifting body--and a white-haired stranger wielding a hammer. Over one breath-snatching night the teens are hurled into a black-market fossil racket stretching from Kimberley mangroves to Sydney's harbour arcades. With Abba's wise-cracking grandfather, a curse-casting elder and a traumatised pearl diver at their backs, the friends must decide what matters most: justice for a murdered man, or their own survival. Set against cyclone skies and ghost-lit cemeteries, *Dinosaur Murder* is a coming-of-age adventure where courage is measured in footfalls, friendship--and fossilised steps that can never be replaced.

Publisher: https://www.writers-exchange.com/dinosaur-murder/

# Giant Stolen Cheesecake

## {Mid-Grade Reader (Primary School Aged)}

*Twelve-year-old Strobe Bevan-Evans only wanted new blades and a trick to impress her snobby classmates. She never expected to chase a one-metre cheesecake--and a pair of art thieves--at ninety kilometres an hour.*

When Aunt Olwyn's spectacular engagement banquet ends in disaster, the social pages blame Olwyn for the vanished dessert...and four priceless paintings. To clear her aunt's name, Strobe teams up with pizza-delivery blader Winston Wong, camera-mad Alex Wong, and accounting prodigy Tran Nuen.

From half-pipes and city traffic to a frantic airport showdown, the kids flip, grind and custard-chucker their way through a mystery packed with laughs, friendship and guts.

*Can one fearless skater and three loyal friends turn the city upside-down before the real thieves escape--cheesecake crumbs and all?*

Publisher: https://www.writers-exchange.com/giant-stolen-cheesecake/

# Outcast Trilogy

{Young Adult Fantasy}

*For centuries the Eastern Zoners have scavenged the poisoned wastelands surrounding Megalopolis while the gene-perfect Megas rule in glittering towers behind five glass walls. Fish--an unwanted Mega throwback with white hair and emerald eyes--should never have lived past infancy. Ari--an over-chipped Mega girl--should have been thrown from the Ritual Pier. Weed--scarred by a golden-clawed bear--speaks futures he cannot remember. Branch--small, fierce, and fearless--breaks bones for sport.*

*Thrown together by prophecy, betrayal, and an approaching techno-cult called the Oriacans, the four outcasts must cross deserts, slave mines, and volcanic fields, survive an arena of death, and challenge the very idea of what it means to be human. If they fail, Megalopolis will burn and every Zone will fall. If they succeed, the Rule Changer will rewrite the world.*

## Book 1: Outcast

Fish was born wrong: white-haired, green-eyed, too tall--part Mega, part Zoner, unwanted by both worlds. On the night he rescues Ari from a twenty-storey fall, he forges a bond that will shake an empire. With prophecy-scarred Weed and battle-hungry Branch, Fish crosses gas pits, slave camps, and the bone-littered Arid Zone, chased by hunters who believe throwing him back on the rubbish heaps will keep their perfect city safe.

Yet every rule is just a chain--until someone strong enough breaks it.

Publisher: https://www.writers-exchange.com/outcast/

## Book 2: The Punisher

The Mighty Arena devours heroes. Fish intends to walk out alive. But the price of victory is steep: out-fight a slaver called Thief, outwit a swan-masked tyrant, and out-play the Punisher herself--while Branch bleeds and Weed's visions grow darker than the volcanic sky. One wrong move and thirty prisoners feed the sworcs. Two wrong moves and the Rule Changer dies before he changes anything.

Publisher: https://www.writers-exchange.com/the-punisher/

## Book 3: Rule Changer

War drums echo across five Zones. In their path stands one scavenger boy who was never meant to live. Fish must bargain with mountain spirits, persuade enemies who carved his back with whips, and protect Ari while her damaged brain fights the Knowledge Chips' fail-safe. Behind them lurches a god made of glass and fire. Ahead lies a decision no prophecy foretold: what rules must stay broken, and which ones must rise in their place?

Publisher: https://www.writers-exchange.com/rule-changer/

# The Mask

{Young Adult Thriller}

The Grand Canal dazzles beneath winter fireworks, yet danger prowls its labyrinth of bridges and tunnels.

Dragged to Italy while his engineer father helps "save" a sinking city, Rob Vian longs for Australian beaches--until a skeleton-masked stranger tries to hurl him into a moon-black canal. Luca, the hotel-keeper's fearless daughter, insists it's only Carnevale mischief. But when the masked stalker returns, their game turns deadly.

From secret family trees to a marble palace abandoned for centuries, Rob and Luca uncover riddles buried since the Black Plague--riddles that whisper of lost fortunes, broken promises and a contessa no one has seen in years.

Carnival ends in eight nights. By then Rob must solve the puzzle, rescue a kidnapped violinist and expose a murderer--or become the festival's final victim.

Publisher: https://www.writers-exchange.com/the-mask/

# We Are Tam

{Mid-Grade Science Fiction}

Mirror-images aren't supposed to talk--let alone beg for help. When fourteen-year-old Tamarisk "Tam" Woodward collapses during PE class, she blames a migraine…until a translucent girl steps out of thin air. Tameron, Tam's exact double from the 25th century, is desperate: her father Darwei has vanished into a forbidden time-coma, and the ruthless Elders are erasing every trace of the past.

Joined by Tam's quick-witted brother Steven, the girls chase clues across modern-day Sydney, the eerie ruins of Oldcit, and a glittering future city where night-lights banish darkness--and truth. From code-filled cylinders to stone sphinxes guarding hidden tunnels, every discovery tightens the clockwork that binds their two worlds.

But history has teeth. Snow-white mosquitoes patrol frozen streets, and one wrong step could turn Tam into a statue forever…

Can two teens, one scientist and a cantankerous professor rewrite destiny before six centuries shatter for good?

Publisher: https://www.writers-exchange.com/we-are-tam/

## You can find ALL our books on our website at:

*http://www.writers-exchange.com*

## All our Young Adult Novels:

*https://www.writers-exchange.com/category/genres/young-adult/*

## All Patricia's Books:

*http://www.writers-exchange.com/Patricia-Bernard/*